UMBRELLA
MOUSE
to the
RESCUE

Praise for *The Umbrella Mouse*

'Move over *War Horse* ... an enchanting first novel' *Telegraph*

'An ambitious and wonderfully well-achieved first novel'
Michael Morpurgo

'A spellbinding tale of bravery and hope, where courage is
found in the smallest of heroes' Gill Lewis, author of *Sky
Hawk*

'An exquisite children's book' *Telegraph*, 50 Best Books of
2019

'Brims with courage, friendship and adventure' *Bookseller*

'A stunning debut novel' *Oldie*

'The wartime background is vivid and completely convincing
and Pip and her animal comrades are beguiling characters'
lovere

Also by Anna Fargher

The Umbrella Mouse

UMBRELLA MOUSE

MOUSE

to the

RESCUE

ANNA FARGHER

ILLUSTRATED BY SAM USHER

MACMILLAN
CHILDREN'S BOOKS

First published 2020 by Macmillan Children's Books
an imprint of Pan Macmillan
20 New Wharf Road, London N1 9RR
Associated companies throughout the world
www.panmacmillan.com

ISBN 978-1-5290-0399-4

Text copyright © Anna Fargher 2020
Illustrations copyright © Sam Usher 2020

1 3 5 7 9 8 6 4 2

A CIP catalogue record for this book is available from the British Library.

Printed and bound by CPI Group (UK) Ltd, Croydon CR0 4YY

To Marie-Madeleine Fourcade and her children,
Christian and Béatrice, Noah's Ark, Nancy Wake and
all the animals who fight for the lives of human beings.

CHAPTER ONE

FAREWELL TO THE FALLEN

A dense summer wind sighed across the forest in Normandy, rippling the oak leaves above Noah's Ark's hideout, which was now inside a rabbit warren buried deep beneath the trees, near the eastern border of the Normandy forest. Below a crimson sky crowding with tall slate clouds, Pip hung her head with the rest of Noah's Ark as they followed Madame Fourcade across the dusty, parched earth. A rumble of thunder rolled in the distance and the undergrowth rustled as if excited for the long-awaited rain to arrive.

The animals left the warren behind them, Madame Fourcade the hedgehog padding ahead with Rémi the swallow, waddling on his talons beside her. Pip had seen him visit Madame Fourcade once before, and, although Madame Fourcade never revealed what they spoke of, her energy made Pip sure Rémi had brought news of her

1

hoglets who had been in hiding since the start of the war. The swallow's slim, streamlined body had long, pointed wings, arcing elegantly behind him over a lean forked tail, and his iridescent feathers shimmered as he spoke to Madame Fourcade in furtive whispers. Reaching a place where a scarlet gloom swirled above a gap in the treetops, the hedgehog turned and thanked him with a smile, and the swallow bowed his inky head to his throat. He spread his wings and flashed his white underbelly as he leaped into the air and disappeared through the trees.

The animals came to a standstill, and Pip stared at the acorn she carried in her paws. Turning its cool, unremarkable shell, she watched its smooth surface gleam. Its hat was the same colour and texture as the ancient oak tree looming beside her. Its rugged trunk was twisted and gnarled with deep crevices, like wrinkles etched into the oldest skin.

'*Mes amis*, both new and old,' Madame Fourcade began, cradling two acorns of her own, and the animals looked up at her. 'Four weeks have passed since the battle at the Nacht und Nebel camp, and although our wounds are healing with each day that goes by our scars will never disappear. For each one changes us forever and tells a story we carry with us for the rest of our lives.'

Pip peered up at the hedgehog and saw that the scabs where barbed wire had scored her face had now been replaced with pearly lines. Shuddering with the memory of the night they had escaped, she looked away and her eyes travelled to the newest members of Noah's Ark, whose broken tails and ragged ears had also healed since their rescue.

'When we lose those we care for,' Madame Fourcade continued, 'our spirits suffer and mend over time like our skin. But we cannot see these scars; only grief reminds us of them. It's time for us to say farewell to our dear friends, Hans, Léon and GI Joe, and give our hearts the remedy to heal.'

Every day since their escape, Noah's Ark had watched the forest, hoping the rat, the eagle and the messenger pigeon would return. At first, every ear pricked at the distant flap of wings or shudder of ground ferns, but, as time wore on, the animals stopped turning their heads to the normal sounds of the forest. Even Pip, who had raced to investigate every snap of a twig or flutter of leaves had slowly lost faith, finding each fruitless search a disappointment more difficult to bear.

'*Great oaks from little acorns grow,*' Madame Fourcade said, smiling sadly. 'In this huge world so full of creatures big and small we may feel as tiny as these acorns, but with brave hearts we can become as mighty as these trees. We are never the same after we lose the ones we love, but the dead will never die if they are not forgotten.'

Pip nodded, feeling the sting of tears in her eyes as she remembered her Mama and Papa. Not a day had gone by that she hadn't thought of them and their last wish to take their family umbrella to the museum in Italy, where her mother had come from a long line of umbrella mice. Pip's father, like Pip, had grown up inside the umbrella shop in London. But war had taken them from her and now she hoped her parents would understand her decision to stay with Noah's Ark and fight until the conflict was over. They were weaker without Léon, Hans and GI Joe. It was her fault they were gone and they needed her help.

'With these acorns,' the hedgehog continued, 'we remember their sacrifice: the greatest that war can possess. May their roots spread far so that their leaves graze the clouds, and forever mark their strength and courage.'

Pip and Madame Fourcade placed their acorns on the forest floor and the hedgehog burrowed into the ground beside them while the members of Noah's Ark watched with their whiskers drooping on their cheeks.

'For Léon, who saved my life and others in Noah's Ark.' Madame Fourcade's voice cracked as she placed his acorn inside the hole and buried it. 'He was the most gallant eagle that ever was and we shall never forget him.'

Silence descended as the animals hung their heads in remembrance of him. Fiercely protective with golden eyes and strong speckled wings that dwarfed her tiny frame, Pip had been so frightened of Léon at first. But his tenderness, wisdom and bravery soon outshone her fear and her heart weighed heavily as she remembered his last moments.

After a long pause, Madame Fourcade carried the next acorn a few paces and Noah's Ark watched solemnly as she dug the earth beside it.

'For our dear American ally, GI Joe, the fastest

messenger pigeon in Churchill's Secret Animal Army. You came to our aid in our darkest hour with a heart of gold and the gift of laughter when we had forgotten how to smile. We thank you for your unfaltering courage,' Madame Fourcade continued, placing the next acorn in its grave, and dragging soil into the hole. 'And we share your woe for your mate, Lucia, who took advantage not only of your kindness, but also of our need for help, and betrayed us all. She reminded us that a friend can be a traitor and we will never make the same mistake again.'

Lucia, the white messenger pigeon and secret Nazi spy, had sabotaged Noah's Ark from within. She had revealed her true nature when she attacked them all with the Goliath Rats and sentry owls in the escape from the Nacht und Nebel camp, and Pip felt ashamed that she had once admired her. Lucia was beautiful and daring, and Pip had been delighted when the pigeon had wanted to be her friend. She shivered, remembering the pigeon's cold, waxy talons closing around her when she'd tried to snatch Pip away.

'We bury this last acorn in memory of Hans, the German resister fighting with Churchill's Secret Animal Army for the better life of all,' the hedgehog went on, padding forward to a place that created an even triangle between the three graves. 'We knew him only briefly yet he showed us a true, heroic nature and we are proud to have fought alongside him.'

Pip stepped forward and as Madame Fourcade met her gaze the hedgehog understood what stirred in Pip's heart. Passing the acorn to her, she joined the rest of Noah's Ark surrounding the little mouse, their brows creased with mourning.

Pip's eyes filled with tears as she thought of Hans. She'd first met him in London with Dickin the search-and-rescue dog just after she'd lost her parents and her beloved umbrella shop, all destroyed by a flying bomb. From that moment on, he'd never stopped protecting her and he'd promised to take her to the umbrella museum in Gignese before returning to Germany to fight the enemy from within.

Pip sank her paws into the cold earth and dug a hole in silence, but as she covered Hans's acorn with soil she was unable to stifle a whimper of sorrow, and together Noah's Ark cried softly all around her.

'We have waited for our friends who would never return.' Madame Fourcade sighed. 'Our scouts have had no word of their capture, and although we are still grieving we must continue to help the humans end this war. Yesterday,

I received word from London Headquarters, and, now that we have rested and hidden long enough after the escape from the camp, it is time for us to resume our work and move on.'

Pip and Noah's Ark nodded sadly, knowing the hedgehog was right.

'The human Allied armies are advancing from the north and west of France and many more soldiers are expected to invade the southern coast any day. This means they are pushing the enemy back east to Berlin from all sides and the Allied army is nearing Paris. Its liberation will symbolize the coming freedom for France! This is our chance to win our country back!'

The animals began muttering to one another and Pip's stomach stirred with both elation and melancholy. When she first came to France, she had intended to press on with her journey to Italy and she never imagined how important Madame Fourcade and her troop of animals would become. Not only had they saved her life, but they'd been the best friends she had ever known and the thought of saying goodbye to them at the end of the war made her heart ache.

'Bernard Booth has ordered us to help the civilian uprising in the city,' Madame Fourcade went on, and at once Henri the stag's ears flattened. 'To do so, we must find the white mouse hiding beneath the human's feet inside the catacombs. She is another member of Churchill's Secret Animal Army and she is fighting with the Resistance there in Paris. Together, we'll rise up and weaken the enemy. Come, let us prepare for our journey to the City of Lights!'

Murmuring, Noah's Ark trod after Madame Fourcade towards the warren, but, as Pip turned to follow, the upper boughs of the trees to her right rustled. Instantly, the fur on the back of her neck stood on end, urging her to look over her shoulder.

Pip gasped. A black shape was hurtling through the trees towards them.

CHAPTER TWO

THE INTRUDER

'Madame Fourcade!' Pip cried as she raced after her friends. 'Something's coming!'

Suddenly, cracking wood echoed in the forest and Noah's Ark whipped their heads towards the sound and cowered in alarm, spying a black shape tumble through the air and crash into the ground ferns below, just a short distance from where the animals were standing.

'What was that?' a rabbit asked, thumping the ground with his hind leg.

'Everyone stay completely still,' Madame Fourcade hushed, prickles bristling all over her body. 'Slowly take cover under whatever you can,' she whispered, 'and do not huddle together in the warren – spread out! All our work will be lost if everyone is captured.'

Thunder boomed as Noah's Ark scurried under the low

ferns and thick brambles tangled across the forest floor.

'We'll investigate,' a squirrel said, scaling a nearby tree trunk with another squirrel chasing her from behind. Bounding across the lofty branches, they peered into the undergrowth with flicking tails. 'It looks like a crow, Madame.'

'Is it moving?' whispered the hedgehog as loudly as she could. Pip stretched up on her tiptoes, but she saw only the forest swaying in the wind.

'We can't be sure,' the other squirrel answered, jumping to another branch and peering from a different angle. 'It's covered by the undergrowth.'

'Rabbits – come with me and Henri.' Madame Fourcade's eyes blazed. 'Tread lightly and be careful not to be seen.'

'Wait for me!' Pip dashed to them. The three rabbits gazed at the hedgehog with their ears twitching warily upon their heads.

'Fine.' Madame Fourcade sighed, knowing there was nothing she could do to stop her. 'Henri and I will be right behind you.'

A rabbit offered his front paw for Pip to climb and she darted up his shoulder to sit at the back of his neck. Beside them, Henri the stag dipped his head to the ground and Madame Fourcade clumsily clambered up his nose and scaled the length of his face to stand between his ears.

'Go!' Madame Fourcade whispered, towering above them from Henri's full height. 'And be ready to run as fast as you can.'

The rain arrived and thudded through the forest as the rabbits crept forward, brushing the undergrowth away with their noses and padding softly on their long, powerful legs. The fallen bird's stark black shape inched into view, lying lifelessly on its stomach with its head flopped on one wing, splayed out on a bed of battered ferns.

'Is it dead?' Pip asked, staring at the black bird's nearly closed eyes, gleaming with slivers of gold.

'Shhhhh,' Madame Fourcade hushed as the stag stepped quietly beside them. The three rabbits edged closer, their paws poised to race away.

'It's a little small for a crow,' Henri whispered, nudging the bird with his nose. He grimaced as its acrid smell rushed up his nostrils.

'Whatever it is,' the hedgehog said, gazing into the treetops, 'we can't stay in the open like this for much longer. It could be a trap.'

The animals looked into the forest with their hackles rising. The rest of Noah's Ark had vanished into the thick undergrowth and Pip swallowed, wondering what else could be watching them from hiding places they did not know of.

'We can't just leave it here,' Pip said, nerves jangling as she slid from the rabbit's back to the forest floor and approached the bird. It looked harmless, as though it were just sleeping with its beak open, and Pip's ears pricked, waiting to hear a snore. 'If it's in trouble, we should do something.'

'It's dead,' one of the rabbits said, prodding its limp wing with its paw. 'There's nothing we can do.'

'Come,' Madame Fourcade said, 'this soul is beyond our help.'

'Wait,' Pip said, staring at its thin, bony chest, willing it to rise and fall. Its tattered feathers hung from its fragile body and her stomach clenched, catching its sour stench in her nose. As she stared at its eyes for a flicker of life, thunder clapped above the trees and the rain fell heavier through the forest. 'I'm sorry,' she said, gently stroking the bird's listless head, 'I hope you didn't suffer too much.'

'Don't touch it!' Madame Fourcade snapped, quills dripping with water. 'It might be diseased.'

Pip snapped her paw away, a strange black dust clinging to her palm. A plump raindrop landed on the bird and trickled down its neck, exposing a trail of shimmering green and purple feathers.

'Let it rest in peace,' the hedgehog said firmly. 'It could have been sent to draw us away from our hideout. It's time to return to the warren – *now*!'

It was then that the black bird's eyes snapped open, burning bright amber and Pip and the others stumbled backwards in fright, watching its haggard body heave.

'Liddle lady?' The black bird coughed. 'I thought you'd be in the Italian umbrella museum by now.'

'GI Joe?' Pip's mouth fell open in disbelief and she

rushed to his side. 'Is that you?'

'*Mon dieu!*' Madame Fourcade gasped.

'Yes,' GI Joe replied weakly. 'Thank God I've found you. I've been looking all over the forest. I've searched every hideout I'd seen you use before. I remember this cluster of oak trees being damned hard to find.'

Pip's heart danced behind her ribs. If GI Joe was alive, didn't that mean Léon and Hans could be too?

Henri dipped his head to the ground and the hedgehog hurried to Pip, who was cradling the pigeon's head on her lap while the rabbits looked on with their whiskers drooping on their cheeks.

'GI Joe,' Madame Fourcade asked urgently, 'what happened to you?'

'There's no time,' the pigeon panted. The raindrops fell faster and heavier, and rinsed the soot from his feathers in uneven stripes of black and grey. 'They're coming for you.'

'Who?' Pip squeaked.

'The Milice.'

'The French Resistance hunters,' a rabbit gasped, thudding his hind leg with fear.

'They're searching all over Normandy for the Umbrella Mouse. They want revenge for Noah's Ark's escape from the camp.'

15

Pip's breath halted in her throat.

'Lucia,' Henri growled, puffing air angrily out of his nose, 'she must have told them everything.'

'Thank whiskers we moved Noah's Ark from the hollow to the rabbit warren when we did. Is Lucia alive, GI Joe?' Madame Fourcade asked firmly. 'Tell us what happened after the fire.'

'There's no time,' he said, struggling to speak. 'A swarm of Butcher Birds is coming for you.'

'Butcher Birds?' Pip swallowed.

'Great grey shrikes with black masks,' he panted. 'Now go! Run! Before it's too late!'

With that, the pigeon's eyes rolled into the back of his head and his body fell limp against the forest floor in a faint.

'Rabbits,' said Madame Fourcade, and they stood to attention at once. 'Hurry back to the warren and warn the others!' A fork of lightning fractured the sky as the rabbits' white, fluffy tails vanished into the trees. 'Pip, let GI Joe go so Henri can scoop him up.'

The stag bent his head to the ground and carefully directed his antlers beneath GI Joe's fragile body, guiding him on to three hooks in Henri's horns.

'Now you two,' Henri said, resting his chin on the

ground, and Pip and Madame Fourcade clambered up his face to stand between his ears, cocking warily in every direction. 'And hang on tight.'

'Wait!' Pip cried. 'The umbrella! I can't leave it in the warren – I have to go back for it!' Her stomach twisted with guilt that she didn't have it with her. If anything happened to it, she would be betraying Mama and Papa's memory and all the other Hanway mice who had lived in it before her.

'Stay where you are, little one,' said Henri, abruptly rocking on his front knees to stand at his full height, 'the warren may not be far away, but I'm faster than you'll ever be.'

Leaping forward, Henri galloped through the undergrowth to where Noah's Ark scrambled around the rabbit warren, preparing to leave. Pip saw two squirrels emerge from her and Madame Fourcade's burrow with the umbrella raised above their heads.

'Noah's Ark!' Madame Fourcade yelled, speaking as quickly as she could. 'The Butcher Birds are coming and a fate worse than death awaits us if we are caught by them.' The animals' ears flattened, and they muttered fearfully to one another as they hopped over to the stag. 'Go in small groups of four or five if you must,' the hedgehog continued

17

gravely. 'Any more than that and we risk too many of us being killed or captured.'

'What if they find us?' a beaver asked from the middle of the group beside his wife and son.

'Everyone knows the Butcher Birds never stop hunting until they get what they want,' a tabby cat added.

'Remember that if you are found they will try everything to convince you to share your secrets so you must escape by whatever means you can. But if you are caught you must be strong – no matter how much pain they inflict, you cannot breathe a word about us. You'll be killing us all if you reveal our secrets. If you speak, it must only be with lies.'

'Where do we go now?' Robert the bullfinch's brow furrowed as he hurriedly strapped Noah's Ark's small crystal radio set to his back.

'Paris, as planned. We must find the white mouse by entering the catacombs via a secret entrance below a statue of an angel in the Luxembourg Gardens. Once inside, turn right and keep going straight, then you won't get lost inside the labyrinth of limestone quarries beneath the city. Bernard Booth says it stretches for hundreds of miles.'

'But, Madame –' Henri shook his head as the rest of Noah's Ark nodded and collected into their small groups of four or five animals – 'a stag cannot enter the catacombs or fight on the streets of Paris. I will come with you as far as I can, then will remain in the forest and wait for your return.'

'And we will meet again with victory singing in our hearts, *mon cher ami*.' Madame Fourcade smiled. 'Everyone: sabotage the enemy every chance you get on the way!' the hedgehog continued, and Noah's Ark listened with their ears pricked high. 'Keep your eyes and ears open, and your noses to the ground – above all, trust no one. We cannot be sure which animals are Axis or Allied, but we *can* be sure the Milice will leave no stone unturned. We'll reunite in Paris in a few days and fight for our liberation together! Now split up and get away from here as fast as you can!'

Noah's Ark scattered in all directions with many glancing back over their shoulders for final glimpses of Pip and Madame Fourcade standing between Henri's ears before they disappeared into the tree canopy or vanished through the ground ferns.

'There must be something we can do for GI Joe,' Pip said, staring up as Henri scooped the umbrella into his upper antlers above the pigeon, who flopped listlessly in the stag's horns. 'We can't lose him now. He needs a doctor.'

'He needs more than that.' Madame Fourcade's brow furrowed. 'He needs a miracle.'

'We must take him to the Great Stag,' Henri said

firmly. 'His ancient knowledge of forest medicines is the only thing that can save GI Joe. Our forest is large, but now we're in the eastern region, and the Great Stag isn't far. He's always been based to the south-east and I'm sure his small band of Resistance fighters will help us when we tell them how much GI Joe has helped the cause.'

'That's if the Great Stag is still alive,' Madame Fourcade replied. 'Rogue Wolves moved into his territory not long ago. They answer to no one and they serve nothing but nature itself. Most of the wolves in that part of the forest were our allies, but the Rogues have been killing them in droves, using the sloping ground there to hide, ambush and kill anyone outside their own packs. Then they take their land for themselves. Without help from other wolves, we will not be protected, and if the Rogue Wolves catch our scent before we find the Great Stag we're finished.'

'But we have to try,' Pip said, her tail flicking with determination. 'GI Joe would do anything to help us if we were him. He'd never be afraid of the Rogue Wolves and nor should we. He's risked everything to save us from the Butcher Birds – we must do the same for him too.'

'You're right, *chérie.*' Madame Fourcade sighed. 'But we only stand a chance if you sprint, Henri. If the Butcher Birds don't get us first, the Rogue Wolves will. And the sooner we get GI Joe help, the sooner we will reach Paris.'

'I only know where his territory lies.' Henri hung his head. 'I don't know where his hideout is.'

'Then we must hope we still have friends in those parts,' Madame Fourcade said. 'The Great Stag has resisted the enemy since the beginning of the war and his group operates there somewhere near brambles. Our squirrels and birds have communicated with his scouts in the past. He sends bees and bats – they were the ones to tell us the Rogue Wolves had arrived in their territory. They'll be keeping a lookout for danger, just like we do. If they approach, we will reveal who we are with the Resistance's secret phrases. GI Joe does not have time for games.'

'But what if the Butcher Birds catch up with us before we find them?' Pip asked, staring warily into the treetops.

'This forest is dense,' the hedgehog said. 'If all else fails, we will hide and do everything we can not to be found.'

'Then hurry, Henri.' Pip swallowed. 'We have to get him help before it's too late.'

CHAPTER THREE

GABRIEL AND MADELEINE

Pip and Madame Fourcade gripped the fur on the crown of Henri's head as he raced through the blustering wind and rain, plummeting through the forest. On and on he ran, weaving around tall trunks and shrubs until at last the Great Stag's territory of undulating slopes appeared, rolling into the distance for as far as they could see.

Henri picked up speed and descended the first decline. Reaching the sodden earth below and swerving sharply to the right, he galloped between the rises of the land, sheltering behind them so as not to be seen from higher ground.

'We must move faster or the wolves and the Butcher Birds will be upon us, Henri!' Madame Fourcade cried, shaking the storm from her quills as Henri slowed, thick mulch now clinging to his hooves.

'I'm trying,' the stag panted, stumbling through the sludge.

'We need to get out of this muck,' Pip said, looking around her, with raindrops dripping from her whiskers. 'Climb that slope!' She pointed to a bank on their left where a steady stream of water trickled down its surface and soaked the earth below.

'But there's no cover up there.' Henri shook his head. 'If the Rogue Wolves or Butcher Birds don't see us first, then men will.'

'Men are slower than wolves and Butcher Birds,' Madame Fourcade said.

'Their bullets are faster than all three, Madame.'

'We have to take that risk if we are going to save GI.'

'You can do it, Henri,' Pip said, tenderly stroking the fur between his ears. 'I know you can.'

'As you wish.' Henri sighed, puffing heavily as he crested the bank with his ears cocking for sounds of the enemy. 'Hold tight!'

The air grew dense with thunder as Henri rushed forward. Now with firm ground beneath him, he raced on, vaulting over fallen branches and weaving around clusters of trees. The heat rose from his body as Pip clutched at his fur, and she bit her lip with worry, staring up at GI Joe and the umbrella jostling in his antlers.

As a bolt of lightning raked across the dark morning sky and illuminated the forest in a strange violet glow, Pip's eyes were drawn to a powerful shape bounding on all fours, flickering behind the tree trunks below. Turning her head to the opposite side of the bank, she spied another, matching Henri's speed.

'Wolves!' Madame Fourcade's eyes rounded with fear, seeing their huge, sinewy bodies tear through the trees towards them. 'Run, Henri!'

Henri's hooves charged across the ground and the wolves curled their lips back from white pointed teeth as a chilling howl swallowed the forest whole.

'They're gaining on us!' Pip cried, glancing behind them. Three wolves were giving chase and drooling, smelling the scent of fear on the wind.

'Keep going!' Madame Fourcade urged. 'Don't let them circle us!' But the wolves drew closer and enveloped the stag from the rear. Feeling their warm breath panting on his heels, Henri leaped sharply to the right, bucking his hind legs out behind him and struck a wolf in the muzzle. It yowled and crumpled in pain. A moment later, another wolf collided with it and they tumbled down the hill, snarling at each other's throats.

'We have to do something,' Pip said, panicked, listening to Henri's breath rasp with fatigue.

'All we can do is run.' The hedgehog trembled beside her as the wolves relentlessly sprinted forward, gnashing their jaws at the stag. 'Only luck can decide our fate now.'

A shard of lightning flashed above the trees and the stag hurried onwards, gaining a few valuable strides. But a moment later Pip and Madame Fourcade gasped with dread, seeing a large fallen trunk blocking the path ahead.

'Hang on!' Henri panted, and Pip and Madame Fourcade held their breath as he hurled himself into the air. Grazing its bark with his hooves, the stag cleared the fallen tree and landed heavily on the other side with GI Joe and the umbrella rocking precariously in his horns.

'Look out!' Madame Fourcade shrieked.

Pip yelped with horror. Ahead, a huge white wolf charged straight for them. A smaller grey wolf sprinted beside it and Pip shivered, feeling its silver gaze bore into her own.

'We're surrounded!' Henri bellowed, swiftly zigzagging and darting his head from left to right in search of a place to run, but the wolves were everywhere and nearing every second. 'Hold tight!' he yelled, and with a defiant puff of his nose, he lowered his head of horns to attack.

'Henri, no!' Pip cried as Madame Fourcade curled her prickles around her paws, still clinging to Henri's fur. 'GI Joe and the umbrella will get hurt!'

'Forgive me!' Henri said, hurtling towards the white and grey wolves, zooming closer with every stride. 'This is our only hope!'

Pip couldn't breathe. There was no escape. Sharp teeth snapped from all sides and the wolves' pants echoed in her ears like a rhythmic chant, increasing in hunger and speed as they closed in on their prey. With no time to think and nowhere to run, Pip scrunched up her eyes and hoped.

The white wolf and his mate pounced and a fearful roar enveloped them all. Yet Henri raced onwards with his hooves pounding the earth even faster than before. Snarls sounded behind them, and Pip and Madame Fourcade dared to look back at the wolves who were now somersaulting across the forest floor.

'The white wolf and his mate must be our allies!' Pip cried, relief flooding through her as they edged further from the fray. 'That must be why they are helping us!'

'We can't be sure of that,' Madame Fourcade added gravely. 'Any stranger could be fighting for the enemy. We'll only know which side they're on when we speak.'

'And we can't risk mistaking them,' Henri puffed, slowing to a canter and catching his breath before struggling to pick up speed once more. 'We must keep going!'

The stag bounded forward in exhausted strides and Pip couldn't take her eyes off the wolves, gnashing their fangs at one another's throats. The white wolf dwarfed the others, and with the help of his mate soon the three smaller wolves retreated into the distant trees with their grey, bushy tails tucked between their legs.

'They've beaten them!' Pip gasped, a chill rippling over them when the white wolf and its mate threw their heads back in triumph and howled over the storm.

'Hurry, Henri,' Madame Fourcade said urgently as their haunting chorus ceased. 'It won't be long before—'

'They're coming after us!' Pip quailed, the wolves' steely gaze turning to her. 'Run!'

'Stay where you are!' the white wolf barked, racing after the stag with his mate.

'Henri!' Madame Fourcade looked fearfully over her shoulder. 'Don't stop until we can be sure they are our allies. They won't attack us if they are friends.'

Pip glanced up at GI Joe and the umbrella cradled in Henri's horns, and bit her lip.

'Foolish creatures!' the grey wolf growled as Henri sprang forward, his whole body trembling with the toll of the chase. 'Stop now if you want to live!'

Thunder crashed above the animals as the white wolf charged down the bank to the foot of the slope and dashed ahead with spots of black rainwater spattering his snowy fur.

'Run!' Madame Fourcade cried. 'Don't let him attack us from the front!'

'Don't give up, Henri!' Pip yelled, dread knotting inside her as the stag desperately competed with the wolves, edging ahead of them with fearfully powerful strides. 'Just keep going!'

The white wolf raced back up the bank to their right and leaped for Henri's throat. His fangs glinted in a flash of lightning and Henri reared, pummelling the wolf in the flank with his hooves. The white wolf twisted in the air with a furious snarl and landed on four paws with his mate galloping into the fray from behind.

'Axis or Allied?' the wolves barked, circling the stag with their hackles rising.

'What do you care?' Madame Fourcade spat. 'The Rogue Wolves are neutral – you care about no one but yourselves.'

'The Rogue Wolves are vermin,' the white wolf growled, and the hint of a smile drew across the hedgehog's face, her first test of their loyalties fulfilled. 'If we were like them, we'd have let them feast on you.'

'Wait, Gabriel!' the grey wolf said, her face immediately softening as she noticed the umbrella in Henri's antlers. 'I think . . . it's . . . It's the Umbrella Mouse!'

'We've never heard of the Umbrella Mouse,' Henri panted, rushing at the wolves with his antlers, but they hopped effortlessly out of harm's way. 'And this bird is dead. It is of no—'

'*The blue horse walks on the horizon!*' the white wolf interrupted, with his mate smiling beside him. Madame Fourcade's ears snapped forward and Henri's tail wagged.

'*Under the moon that is full of green elephants,*' the hedgehog replied.

Pip beamed. The wolf and Madame Fourcade had uttered the secret phrases the Resistance used to identify themselves. The hedgehog chuckled as she turned to the wolves, now lolling their tongues out of their mouths like dogs. 'You are right – she is the Umbrella Mouse.'

'Your story has spread far,' the grey wolf said.

'The escape you organized from the Nacht und Nebel camp has crazed the enemy,' the white wolf added. 'The whole forest has been talking about it! I'm Gabriel and this is Madeleine. Consider us your loyal friends.'

'We knew Noah's Ark operated nearby,' Madeleine

added. 'We've been keeping our eyes out for you in the hope we could help you in some way. Your bravery has inspired everyone in the Resistance.'

'What are you doing here?' Gabriel asked as Pip's whiskers drooped with shame. If they'd heard what she'd done, then they'd know it was her fault her friends had been hurt. 'We've sent warnings to other territories ever since the Rogue Wolves forced their way into these woods. We are the only ones left in our pack. They care about nothing except land and prey, and they'll do anything to get it.'

'We're looking for the Great Stag.' Henri stepped forward. 'Our friend is gravely injured and the stag is the only creature who can help him.'

'We know where he is.' Madeleine's tail wagged. 'We've been protecting him since France fell. He isn't far.'

'Please take us there,' Pip said urgently, staring up at GI Joe. 'We don't have much time. We're being hunted by the Milice.'

'We know,' Gabriel said. 'Two days ago we chased the Butcher Birds away from some rabbits near here.'

'They're vicious.' Madeleine pulled her ears back with rage and Pip spotted black scabs where they had been pecked and clawed.

'And they're coming for us now.' Henri's ears cocked. 'I can hear their calls to the west.' Pip shuddered, catching a shrill, shrieking song travelling on the wind.

'Follow us.' Madeleine trotted forward. 'We must be swift if we are going to outrun them.'

The animals hurried down the bank to the right and galloped together up and down rolling slopes across the forest with the Butcher Birds' hunting cries creeping closer through the trees behind them. A few panicked minutes brought them to an abrupt stop at the crest of a hill.

'No!' Madame Fourcade gasped despairingly, seeing a vast tangle of brambles tumbling down the other side of the bank and unfurling into the distant trees.

'We're trapped!' Henri panted, shuffling anxiously on his hooves.

'There's still time.' Pip scowled defiantly. 'Run along this bank, Henri! We'll find a way around the brambles somewhere.'

'Stay where you are!' Madeleine growled, whipping her head round to face the stag, her silver eyes gleaming with authority as she scanned the distant treetops. 'You cannot outrun the Butcher Birds now. They'll be upon us soon.'

The wolves hurried to the thorns and uttered five gruff staccato barks followed by a moan. Instantly a black head with a thick ebony beak popped up from the brambles and hopped into view with a flap of its black-and-white wings.

It perched upon a thorny branch and cocked its head from side to side towards the sound.

'Over here, Pie!' Gabriel barked again. 'We need to see the Great Stag!'

The large magpie darted his gaze to them and, seeing Pip and her umbrella, his eyes widened. Letting out a whistle and a clack, he disappeared again. Seconds later a scratching sounded as the tangle of thorns at their paws shuddered apart, revealing a hidden path slanting deep beneath the web of branches above.

'Come on!' Madeleine bounded forward and at once the animals followed her and Gabriel down the secret passage. As they cleared the entrance, Pip turned to look over her shoulder and watched two tattered badgers drag thick screens of thorns together, and close them inside.

CHAPTER FOUR

THE MAQUIS

Henri rushed forward along a dusty path into a secret glade, descending steeply below a dense roof of brambles. Barbed trunks stretched tall, creating a maze of spiked arches and corridors, veiling them in shadow with only a glimmer of daylight visible through the tangle of branches.

'We need to take cover!' said Pie the magpie urgently as the shrill cries of the Butcher Birds grew louder overhead. 'They'll be scanning the ground for you and they may spot any movement beneath the thorns – follow me!'

Swiftly beating his wings, Pie led them to a place where the brambles enveloped a tall, rotten tree that had collapsed a long time ago against another trunk, forming a large gap beneath. The magpie and the wolves hurried inside and Henri skidded to a halt, his antlers clashing against the bark as he frantically ducked his head and squeezed himself inside.

None of them dared to breathe as they spied the shrikes swarming over the canopy of thorns. One settled upon the brambles above them and cocked its black-masked head, listening for signs of life. Pip trembled beneath, fearing they would hear her heart hammering against her ribs. A long minute passed before it launched into the air again, joining the abattoir of shrikes travelling east through the forest, and the animals sighed with relief as their shrill, shrieking cries faded into the blustering wind.

Pie peered out from under the trunk and launched into the air, leading the way through the maze of brambles again with Henri and the wolves cantering behind. Taking a sharp turn to the left, the animals arrived at the entrance of an earthen cave that gaped from a sheer slope. A large beehive dangled above the opening, and, as the magpie approached with a whistle and a clack, hundreds of bees leaped from their nest, revealing a golden honeycomb beneath.

'Don't worry,' Pie said, landing on Gabriel's back and seeing Henri, Pip and Madame Fourcade's eyes widen in alarm. 'The bees are our scouts and gatekeepers. We know each other well.'

The bees swirled about them, whispering excitedly as their furry claws tickled Pip and the umbrella, then

Madame Fourcade and Henri. But on reaching GI Joe they darted back to their nest with a whirr of unease.

The animals entered the cave, the air inside musty and cool. As daylight faded into the distance behind them, Pip blinked, seeing a yellow-green dot flash before her eyes. Another gleamed in the gloom to her left and a moment later she gaped in wonder as countless little lights glittered all around.

'Fireflies!' Pip said, feeling feet flutter on her outstretched paw.

Rounding a corner, the glow of light intensified with bioluminescent mushrooms growing up the walls, illuminating a cavern under a huge ceiling of roots, with a dozen bats hanging upside down from its woody tendrils.

The Great Stag stood in the centre with a young ermine and a canary on his back. He dwarfed Henri from the size of his hooves to the points on his antlers, decorated with webs of silk shimmering under the light of the fireflies like a ghostly crown. Dangling above his head at the centre of an elaborate pattern was a spider with her legs stretched out in an eight-pointed star.

'Who are you?' The Great Stag scowled, turning to Henri with a stamp of his hoof. His voice was commanding and gruff with age. 'How did you find us?'

'My name is Madame Fourcade,' the hedgehog said, standing tall upon Henri's head. 'I am the leader of Noah's Ark and we have come for your help.'

'Is that *the Umbrella Mouse*?' The Great Stag blinked with disbelief, seeing Pip and the hedgehog, beneath the umbrella cradled in Henri's antlers.

As he padded over to them, the canary and the ermine on his back hurried up his neck to get a better view of the new arrivals from the top of his head, and the bats swung from their perches on the ceiling as their big ears pricked. Pip gazed into the Great Stag's face, greying around his eyes and nose, and swallowed.

'I know you by reputation, of course,' he continued. 'No one has ever freed human and animal prisoners from a camp before – the enemy is incensed! If all Resistance fighters were like you, we'd have rid our country of the invaders a long time ago. I am Gaspard, the head of this small, independent band of Resistance fighters we call the Maquis,' he said, darting his gaze to the other animals in the cavern. 'We have protected this side of the forest for generations.'

'We found them crossing into your territory,' Gabriel the white wolf said, sitting on his haunches.

'And they're lucky we did,' Madeleine said, her silver eyes glistening in the firefly light. 'The Rogue Wolves were about to feed and the Butcher Birds were not far behind.'

'If you have led the Rogue Wolves and the Butcher Birds to our cavern,' Gaspard's voice boomed, 'then you are killing us all! Our size and stealth are the reasons we have never been found and we do not wish to be drawn into a fight we did not start!'

'We got away!' Pip cried, ignoring the blood thudding in her ears. The wolves and the magpie nodded and Gaspard's scowl eased. 'We have come for your help.' She peered up at him, staring down his nose at her. 'Our friend – this pigeon, GI Joe – is gravely ill and we have heard of your knowledge of nature's medicines – it's his only hope.'

'That bird –' the spider frowned, gliding along her webs strung between Gaspard's antlers to get a closer look at the pigeon – 'has the scent and pallor of death.'

'Please . . .' Pip crept forward, clasping her paws against her heart. 'He is one of the bravest members of the Resistance. Without him the whole of Noah's Ark would have been captured by the Butcher Birds and the escape from the Nacht und Nebel camp would never have succeeded.'

'What happened to him?' asked the canary standing between Gaspard's ears as the ermine's nose twitched beside him.

'We're not sure,' Madame Fourcade replied. 'He lost consciousness before he could tell us.'

'We thought he'd died with two more of our friends in the fire at the camp,' Pip said solemnly, her throat tightening with thoughts of Hans and Léon, 'but somehow he survived and flew back to warn us that we were in danger. If he made it out alive, there's a chance our other friends did too, but we may never find out if we lose him now.'

'Very well.' Gaspard sighed. 'Amélie –' he glanced up at the spider hanging from his horns – 'it's your magic, not mine.'

Amélie cast a sail of silk from her body and launched into the air, closing the gap between the stags in an elegant swing between their antlers. A group of fireflies floated to her as she scuttled to GI Joe, and illuminated her eight legs moving feverishly over the pigeon's blackened feathers. Pip, Madame Fourcade and Henri held their breath, hoping that life remained inside their friend.

'He's not as burned as he looks,' Amélie muttered, inspecting his feathers, still unevenly covered with soot. 'He's badly undernourished and dehydrated, but he's alive.' She looked up at Gaspard from GI Joe's listless body. Pip and Madame Fourcade's whiskers pricked upon their cheeks and Henri's tail wagged. 'Barely,' she added, seeing their faces brighten. 'I can't promise we can save him, but we can try.'

'Doing something is always better than doing nothing,' Madame Fourcade said.

'Quickly,' Amélie said, summoning more fireflies with

her top two legs, 'go and gather as much moss you can. Squeeze out the moisture and bring it back here.'

The space darkened as the fireflies' glow swiftly darted to the far reaches of the cavern and disappeared sharply to the right.

'Umbrella Mouse.' Amélie waved down at her, the light of the bioluminescent mushrooms casting her in a dim, green shadow.

Pip clambered up Henri's antlers to crouch beside the spider and GI Joe. 'Pip,' she said, offering her paw to her.

'I hoped we'd meet one day.' Amélie shook it with a smile as the cloud of fireflies returned and floated around Henri's antlers. 'A deeper part of this cavern has a tiny opening on to a marshland filled with sphagnum moss.' Amélie pointed to the fireflies' claws, filled with green sponge. A firefly fluttered to Pip and passed some to her. It was cold and smelt earthy and old. 'It has healed men for hundreds of years, and animals for much longer. When it is woven with my silk, it will absorb any sickness inside his body and hopefully deliver a cure in its place.'

Pip and the fireflies applied the moss to GI Joe's wounds while Amélie climbed upon him and spun it to him with her silk, tightly wrapping him in a bandage filled with medicine, until only his face showed through the weave.

'What happens to him now?' Pip asked, gazing at his cocoon. She couldn't bear the thought of losing him, and shuddered at the pain he must have felt trying to find Noah's Ark and warn them the Milice were coming. He'd saved all their lives at the risk of his own again and she would do anything to give his strength back to him.

Amélie sighed. 'We wait.'

CHAPTER FIVE

SUSPICION

'Now you must answer some questions, Madame,' Gaspard said firmly as the fireflies delivered Amélie back to her web, spiralling between his antlers, and then spread themselves across the cavern like little stars. 'We may have heard of each other, but we are strangers. We've done what you asked, even though you've risked exposing us to the enemy in more ways than one . . .'

'Then let's talk leader to leader,' Madame Fourcade offered, unafraid of his tone. 'The human Allied armies are nearing Paris and the Resistance is preparing to liberate the city. We must help them—'

'Something is far more pressing that that, Madame,' Gaspard interrupted, and the hedgehog's quills stiffened. 'What if your friend has been turned by the enemy? To survive the fire and suddenly reappear at the same time as the Butcher Birds is suspicious, to say the least.'

'Didn't his mate betray your group?' asked the canary perched on Gaspard's head beside the ermine.

'How do you know about Lucia?' Pip frowned, squirming at the thought of her.

'The forest isn't just talking about the Umbrella Mouse,' the canary went on, puffing his chest feathers with confidence. 'Rumours have also spread about the Axis pigeon that attacked Noah's Ark from within. The heart can sway loyalties and your friend's wouldn't be the first. He might be an enemy agent now.'

Pip gazed at GI Joe and wondered if it were possible Lucia could have turned him into an enemy spy, and promptly shook the thought from her head. She'd seen his fury when he'd discovered Lucia's betrayal. He would have killed her before he joined her – Pip was sure of it.

'As far as we know,' Henri said, 'Lucia was killed in the fire along with two other members of Noah's Ark.'

'But now that GI Joe has survived you must question whether she has too,' the ermine remarked.

'No matter how much we admire her for the great escape, the Umbrella Mouse is putting us all in jeopardy.' The canary's feathers ruffled around his neck. 'If the Butcher Birds are closing in, then time is running out before the

Milice catch you and whoever else is by your side. The Maquis are strong because we do not join wider Resistance networks. We should have turned Noah's Ark away and let that pigeon perish from his wounds.'

'How dare you say that!' Pip said furiously, a hot tremor of indignation tingling the fur along her spine. 'GI Joe would never betray us. He was willing to sacrifice his life in the Nacht und Nebel camp and he fought on D-Day for your freedom and mine.' Her eyes narrowed as she looked the yellow bird up and down. 'You should be ashamed of yourself. Show him some respect.'

'You must understand, little one,' Gaspard said gravely, 'the Milice are a merciless organization. They're more dangerous than the Nazis themselves because they're our countrymen. They know our culture and our geography. They blend in easily and they're ruthlessly efficient in crushing anyone resisting the enemy regime.'

'And they'll never stop chasing the Umbrella Mouse,' the canary added. Pip's heart began to thud. 'They know she's the Resistance's treasure. Our scouts are returning every day with reports of the Butcher Birds. Madeleine and Gabriel were attacked and—'

'Enough!' Madame Fourcade yelled. 'There is no hope for our liberation if we fight amongst ourselves. The

Resistance needs to *unite* against the enemy! Not turn on their friends!'

'Alas, none of us is safe from treachery,' Gaspard remarked. 'Anyone connected to you is in danger. Torture dissolves loyalty.'

'Treachery has always been our biggest peril, yet we carry on,' Madame Fourcade cried. 'We must vow never to give information to the invaders – if we're caught, we lie. If we're imprisoned, we escape by whatever means we can.'

'And the enemy is hunting with this intensity, not just because of Pip and wanting revenge for the escape from Nacht und Nebel camp, but because they're scared of her,' Henri added. 'They know they're losing the war now the Allied armies are advancing towards Paris. It's fortunate to have her, not a curse.'

'But the more everyone knows about her, the more danger she is in herself,' Madeleine the grey wolf said. 'She should stay in a small group who can protect her from capture. I am happy to volunteer.'

'Me too.' Gabriel wagged his tail beside his mate.

'Thank you.' Madame Fourcade smiled. 'We appreciate any help you can give us. We'll go now. Then we'll be no threat to the rest of you.'

'No!' Gaspard stamped his hoof. 'I cannot let you leave

before we know what side your friend is on.'

'But he's unconscious!' Pip cried. 'He won't know where he's been or who he's seen.'

'But *you* could talk!' the canary shrieked back. 'Then he'll trap us all!'

Shouts of outrage erupted from Noah's Ark and the Maquis. As their anger reached a bitter din, none of the animals noticed a pair of amber eyes flutter open.

'Liddle lady?' GI Joe blinked groggily. Pip looked down at the pigeon and nearly jumped out of her skin. 'Is that you?'

'Everybody, shhhhh!' Pip yelled over the furore. 'GI Joe's waking up!'

A hush abruptly descended over the animals as the 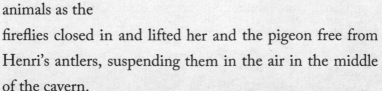 fireflies closed in and lifted her and the pigeon free from Henri's antlers, suspending them in the air in the middle of the cavern.

'Yes, it's me, GI!' Pip beamed, tenderly resting her paws on his cocoon.

'It's good to see you.' He smiled, his voice gruff and sticky with thirst. 'Where are we? How long was I out for? Is it just me or am I seeing stars?'

'They're fireflies,' Henri said softly, watching the pigeon's brow furrow with confusion as he floated in the middle of the cavern. 'We're deep in the forest with another Resistance group, the Maquis.'

'Henri? Is that you, buddy?' GI Joe said, trying to lift his head in the direction of Henri's voice. 'Something's wrong.' His eyes widened with fear. 'I can't move!' Panic seized his voice as he wriggled in his rigid cocoon from side to side. 'What's happened?'

'It's all right, GI,' Madame Fourcade said calmly. 'You're swaddled inside a medicinal bandage . . .'
'Made from a spider's web and sphagnum moss,' Pip added.

'A creepy-crawly and a whosie-what-moss?' The pigeon frowned, and Amélie the spider crossed her upper arms, offended. 'How long have I gotta stay in this thing?'

'For as long as you can stand it,' said Madame Fourcade. GI Joe opened his beak to protest, but the hedgehog silenced him with a stern glance from where she stood on Henri's head and he knew he couldn't argue. 'You saved Noah's Ark from the Butcher Birds. We split up and got out just in time.'

'I'm glad, Madame.' GI Joe sighed with relief.

'The Milice is still patrolling our territory,' said Gaspard, stepping forward and peering at the pigeon. 'We'll know more when our scouts return.'

The pigeon frowned, gawping at the huge stag with the spider hanging from his antlers, and the canary scowling upon his head beside the ermine, standing tall on her hind legs. 'Who are you?'

'My name is Gaspard,' said the Great Stag silkily. 'I'm the leader of the Maquis. I believe it is high time we got to know one another.'

GI Joe's interrogation had begun.

CHAPTER SIX

FRIEND OR FOE?

'He's on our side.' Pip's jaw hardened as she stared into Gaspard's eyes, gleaming ghostly green in the glow of the mushrooms and the fireflies.

GI Joe was silent as his gaze darted to Madame Fourcade.

'We'd ask the same questions had you just arrived at Noah's Ark's hideout without warning,' the hedgehog said, and Pip swallowed, remembering her first meeting with the group after she landed in Normandy with Hans and the umbrella. They hadn't been friendly at all.

'It's all right, kid,' GI Joe cooed softly, reading the furrows on Pip's brow.

'Your friends tell me that you were instrumental in the escape from the Nacht und Nebel camp,' Gaspard said, looking down his nose at the pigeon from his full height.

GI Joe nodded. 'That's correct.'

'And it was the Umbrella Mouse's idea?'

'Yes, sir.'

Pip's chest tightened. Her idea also possibly got Hans and Léon killed, and GI Joe was half dead and exhausted after flying home to save Noah's Ark's lives.

'Was it your mate who betrayed your group,' Gaspard continued coldly, 'and who enabled the capture of your leader and other members?'

'To my shame,' GI Joe said solemnly, and Madame Fourcade and Henri hung their heads. Neither of them had realized she was an Axis spy either. 'Yes, it was.'

'And you had no idea of her plot?' the ermine asked.

'No,' the pigeon said firmly.

'You didn't suspect her at all?' Amélie added, her eight eyes blinking inquisitively. 'How well did you know her?'

'I thought she was as loyal to the Allied cause as I was,' GI Joe cooed. 'We met when she arrived unexpectedly inside my US Army pigeon loft where I was stationed in Italy last year. She had a scroll addressed to our American troops: *Herewith we return a pigeon to you. We have enough to eat.* Her American accent was flawless, her platoon had been wiped out and she was so experienced at delivering messages in combat that the thought never crossed our minds that she was the enemy. After we'd run a few missions together, we grew close. She was orphaned as a chick and raised by human hands – a Nazi pigeon handler, I realize now. She was devoted to him and she could read Man better than anyone I've ever met. But it made her lonely. She'd spent her whole life being an outsider, not feeling like she belonged with humans or animals. She wanted to prove herself and be part of something important. She'd never had anything close to a family, and I felt sorry for her.'

'Oldest trick in the book.' The canary shook his head and GI Joe's amber eyes glazed with remorse.

Pip had never known that about Lucia. She knew she was an orphan, like she was, but she never expected her to have bonded with humans so strongly. Pip had grown fond of Peter, the son of the umbrella-shop owner in London, but she couldn't imagine wanting to belong to his world. Pip's ears flattened. If a Nazi handler and his ways were what drove Lucia, then her heart and mind were lost.

'But how did you both come to be in Noah's Ark if you were stationed with the human army in Italy?' the canary asked, narrowing his eyes in suspicion.

GI Joe glanced at Madame Fourcade. With a soft nod, she permitted him to share his history with the Maquis.

'I've been working for both my human troops and Churchill's Secret Animal Army since the US Army arrived in Great Britain in 1942. I was recruited because of my speed. I deliver messages to Resistance groups when I have leave to rest from my human missions. Noah's Ark and I got to know each other over time and I told Lucia to find them in the forest to the north of the monastery of Bec if she was ever lost or in trouble. I had no doubt that she was an Allied pigeon – I never imagined she'd do what she did. Lucia went missing in action on a human mission in Italy before I left for England to prepare for D-Day. Who knows where she really was? I was broken-hearted and hoped to find her on my next visit to Noah's Ark, but I honestly didn't know if I'd ever see her again. War does that to relationships.'

'So you are responsible for her treachery as much as he is?' Gaspard turned to Madame Fourcade. 'She found Noah's Ark and you invited her in.'

'It's true,' Madame Fourcade replied. 'I was suspicious, but her disguise and her intimate knowledge of GI Joe persuaded me otherwise. She arrived soon after D-Day when Allied pigeons were often sighted. I believed she had come to help us. She was a keen saboteur and a spirited fighter. Like GI Joe, I was fooled and I will never forgive myself for my mistake.'

'How can we trust that you're not harbouring more Axis spies?' Gaspard asked, his gaze flicking to Henri, who glared back at him in the green-lit gloom.

'How can we know that you're not harbouring your own?' Madame Fourcade snapped back. 'As you said, all of us are vulnerable to treachery. Every member of the Resistance has felt the enemy's hunger to destroy us since the Allies won Normandy back. Lucia targeted us as revenge for the French Resistance's role in D-Day's success and for helping the Allied advance towards Germany. Axis agents like Lucia have a vendetta and we are all in danger of capture if we are not careful. Surely you must know that?'

'Which is precisely *why* we are asking you these questions, Madame,' Gaspard flared, and the Maquis eyed one another nervously. Pip held her breath and Henri shifted on his hooves.

'We are on the same side, Gaspard,' Madame Fourcade replied softly, and Pip exhaled as the tension in the cavern eased. 'We are friends, not foes. Let's save our anger for those who deserve it.'

Madame Fourcade and Gaspard stared at one another. In the silent moment that followed, the Great Stag's guard clearly softened before he turned to GI Joe again. 'Did

Lucia survive the fire at the camp?'

GI Joe shook his head. 'I don't know. I woke up in a wheelbarrow filled with charred wood, soot and ash. I don't know how long I'd been there for – I just knew I had to get away as fast as I could.' He craned his neck from inside his cocoon and searched the cavern as best he could. 'Hey, Léon! Hans!' he called. 'Are you in here? Speak up!'

At once, Madame Fourcade and Henri bowed their heads, and Pip's eyes filled with tears. GI Joe took a sharp breath.

'I . . . I . . . thought,' he stammered with dismay. Pip met GI Joe's gaze, but all she could muster was a small shake of her head. The pigeon clenched his jaw and his amber eyes glistened with sorrow. 'It's my fault. If I hadn't been so stupid, she never would have known about you guys.'

'No, GI, it's my fault,' Pip sniffed. 'If I hadn't fallen from Henri's back during the battle, then Lucia wouldn't have snatched me and . . .'

'This war is despicable,' Madame Fourcade growled as Pip covered her face in her paws and wept. 'It *must* end!'

'You're right, Madame.' Gaspard nodded sadly with the Maquis. 'There are just a few more things to clarify, GI Joe. How did you get back here without help? The journey is too far with your injuries to have got here alone.'

'I flew when I could and I hitched rides inside open-topped trucks and farm carts when I couldn't,' GI Joe said wearily, grief clouding his face. 'I was in bad shape. I'd have been finished by a falcon or a human if I'd been seen. I often rested – that's why it took me so long to return to Noah's Ark.'

'And how did you come to know that the Butcher Birds were on the loose?'

'They landed above where I was roosting inside the roof of a barn. I overheard them arguing about their search for the Umbrella Mouse.' GI Joe's voice began to fade, 'I . . . I knew I had to hurry if I was gonna find Noah's Ark in time.'

'Enough of this,' Henri puffed angrily, seeing the pigeon's eyes droop heavily with fatigue. 'He needs sleep and water!'

'He's answered your questions,' added Pip, her tail flicking angrily as GI Joe's head flopped against his cocoon. 'Now leave him alone!'

CHAPTER SEVEN

OPERATION HONEYBEE

Gaspard turned to Madame Fourcade. 'Do you believe him?'

'Yes,' she replied. 'He's the same pigeon I've always known. He hasn't been turned – I'm sure of it.'

'I agree.' Gaspard nodded. 'The resilience he's shown confirms he's your close ally and ours too. Jude,' he said, looking up at the canary perched between his ears. 'Go and collect water from the spring, and nectar from the bees' hive. Our friends deserve some sustenance after the day they've had. Noah's Ark,' Gaspard continued as Jude the canary disappeared into the shadows leading to the beehive, 'I apologize for making you feel unwelcome. I cannot risk having an enemy spy sabotage my network. I agree with you, Madame. The Resistance needs to come together if we are to beat the invaders at this last hurdle. Please think of our hideout as your own. You will be safe here. If you are willing to share information, our combined force will crumble the enemy.'

'*Merci.*' A relieved smile drew across Madame Fourcade's and Henri's lips and the wolves wagged their tails beside them. 'We accept your offer of friendship, but we cannot stay long. We must continue our journey east and get to Paris as soon as possible and help the humans liberate the city.'

Behind them, a low hum gradually increased in volume as seven bees darted into the cavern and delivered acorn shells filled with water and nectar to Pip, Madame Fourcade and Henri. As they savoured them, another bee arrived and buzzed a message into Gaspard's ear.

'Spider webs, sphagnum moss and now honey.' Henri chuckled as Pip carefully aimed a cup of syrup into GI Joe's half-open beak with the help of the fireflies hovering beneath her. 'I told you the Great Stag would know what to do.'

'It wasn't me,' Gaspard said humbly as the bees vanished into the shadows again. 'Amélie, the fireflies and the bees are the experts. Nature's magic comes in many forms and you'll soon see what else it is capable of.'

Pip's ears pricked.

'We are organizing a sabotage mission tonight, if you'd like to join us?' Gaspard asked. 'Your small size and speed is of much value, and we would be honoured to fight alongside you.'

Pip nodded briskly, her whiskers quivering with enthusiasm on her cheeks.

'Wait, *chérie*.' Madame Fourcade's quills bristled slightly. 'Let's find out what they have planned before we dive into danger.'

'My scouts have followed enemy Tiger tanks travelling through the forest,' Gaspard continued, and at once Madame Fourcade's and Henri's ears flattened against their heads. 'Some are a short distance from our brambles, camouflaged in the undergrowth beside the ruins of a castle. We are going to stop them.'

'I saw those metal monsters tear through my home forest like water storming down a river.' Henri shook his head, jostling the umbrella in his horns. 'Tanks are the human's mightiest weapons – and Tiger tanks are the most feared of all.'

Gaspard nodded. '*Oui*, but Allied lives are at risk and our brambles could be crushed if we don't do something.'

'*No* animal can stop them!' Henri stamped his hoof in frustration.

'We have before,' the ermine said proudly, standing between Gaspard's ears.

'What weapons do you have?' Madame Fourcade's brow furrowed. 'Nature can only do so much.'

The ermine grinned. 'Beeswax.'

'Impossible!' Henri flared, and Pip and Madame Fourcade frowned.

'Forgive him.' Madame Fourcade flashed him an authoritative glance. 'Anger is the language of fear.'

'If any of you had come as close to their fury as I have,' Henri added indignantly, 'you would be scared of them too.'

Pip swallowed, remembering the tank they had encountered in the forest on the way to the Nacht und Nebel camp. She could still hear the whistling howl of the shell before it had catapulted her and Henri into the air. She looked at his kind, handsome face and her chest tightened at the memory of him lying unconscious on the ground.

'Our hearts cannot beat without blood pumping through our veins and nor can engines. Some animals can easily puncture their rubber fuel lines,' the ermine explained as she hopped up on to her hind paws and proudly curled her lips back from a row of pointed teeth, framed either side with devilishly long, pointed fangs. 'Then we close the holes again with beeswax and when the engine starts it melts and slowly drains the fuel. The humans don't realize the tanks have been sabotaged until they're already on their journey and an unexpected stop makes them vulnerable to attack.'

'They are lumbering machines,' Gaspard added. 'If they're not prepared, they are unlikely to find cover. And if they can't move they cannot travel to battle. Fewer enemy tanks mean more Allied lives will be saved, and by the time repairs have been made our human armies will have advanced.'

'*Magnifique!*' Madame Fourcade's nose crinkled with delight.

Amélie smiled. 'Our magpie Pie and our ermine Monique have sabotaged a number of Axis tanks, trucks and cars in this way.'

'And they never knew what hit them!' Pie grinned.

'The best part is watching their engines splutter and die.' Monique laughed and Pie nodded. 'The humans always jump up and down with rage.'

'When do we leave?' Pip asked, feeling butterflies in her

stomach. Being surrounded by so many daring adventurers was the best thing to have happened for ages.

'In the hours before dawn,' Gaspard said, 'two of my bat scouts will meet you in the brambles with the beeswax. They'll lead you, Pie and Monique to the tanks and Madeleine and Gabriel will protect you from the Rogue Wolves if they pick up your scent.'

CHAPTER EIGHT

THE TIGER TANKS

Eeriness had consumed the secret bramble tunnels with the setting of the sun, casting tangled silhouettes of snarling thorns against the glittering sky above. Drenched in moonlight, the rustling leaves whispered on the breeze above the ground ferns unfurling into the forest beyond.

After a brief sleep and a meal of honeycomb, nuts and berries, Pie the magpie carried Monique the ermine on his back and led the way out of the Maquis's cavern with Henri, carrying Pip and Madame Fourcade, following closely from behind, and the wolves flanking them on either side. Together, they trotted beneath the beehive still humming with life above the entrance to the cave. As they arrived at the start of their protective bramble maze, two bats carrying rings of beeswax in their mouths dropped from their perches overhead and began to guide the animals through the thorns.

Climbing the steep slope leading back into the forest, Pie cried out in a series of clacks and whistles, and they heard shuffling ahead as shadows scampered across the forest floor. A moment later, the brambles shuddered open and the badger gatekeepers whispered, '*Bonne chance,*' as the animals crested the bank in the open air, sighing in the breeze by the light of the full moon.

'Follow us.' The bats swirled around the animals. 'The tanks are over the hill.'

They headed east through the undergrowth with their ears cocked for danger and Madeleine and Gabriel's eyes gleaming in the gloom. An hour had passed when the ground beneath them grew steep and their pace slowed as they panted on the incline.

'Come on,' the bats encouraged, 'you haven't much further to go.'

Reaching the summit of the hill at last, the animals slowly continued forward until they stopped abruptly behind the last row of trees. The ruins of a small medieval castle stretched above the treetops ahead, silhouetted against a blanket of stars overlooking an enormous valley with a river snaking into the darkness and shimmering in the moonlight. To the south-west, explosions from distant battlefields sparked in the darkness below.

'Over there!' the bats squeaked, twisting upside down and dangling from Henri's horns above the magpie, now perching on the umbrella. Taking the rings of beeswax from their mouths, the bats passed one to Monique, then Pip, and pointed their wings in the direction of some tall shrubs surrounding the castle mound. 'The tanks are hidden under those bushes.'

The wind blustered through the forest as the animals searched the darkness ahead. Sure enough, an unmistakeably man-made row of wheels peered out into the night behind carefully placed leafy boughs freshly cut from nearby trees.

'Listen carefully,' Monique the ermine said, and Pip's ears snapped forward. 'Pie will fly us to the rear of the tanks. I am small and he is big and strong enough to carry us both a short distance. Each one has two fuel compartments – one on the left and another on the right side of the machine. Both are covered with thick metal grates with gaps big enough for you and me to squeeze through. Once we're inside, we'll sabotage the fuel lines with our teeth and plug the holes with beeswax.'

'But you need to act fast,' Pie added, hopping down from the umbrella to meet Pip at the back of Henri's neck.

'The tanks have steel shells that make even the smallest claws clatter and clang. Every time I land on one, the men might hear us. I'll keep watch when you're inside, but the longer you take, the higher the risk we're seen or heard.'

'We'll be keeping watch from here.' Madame Fourcade gave Pip's paw a reassuring squeeze.

'And if we see or hear anything,' Madeleine added, her silver eyes already scanning the darkness, 'we'll howl.'

Gabriel nodded. 'Nothing puts fear into a man like the cry of a wolf.'

'Where *are* the men?' Pip searched the gloom with a twitch of her nose.

'We can't be sure,' Pie whispered. 'They could be in the castle, inside the tanks or camped in foxholes. They sometimes park the tanks over themselves to shield from attacks.'

'But don't worry,' Monique added, seeing Pip's whiskers tremble. 'Human sight and hearing are not nearly as sharp as ours, so we have the advantage.'

'All right.' Pip swallowed, nerves fluttering in her stomach. 'I'm ready.'

'Good girl.' Pie stretched his black-and-white wings.

'Good luck, little one,' Henri whispered, straining his eyes upwards to Pip, who was clutching the magpie's feathers and climbing on to his back.

'Keep your ears pricked for our warning, *chérie*,' Madame Fourcade said, 'and remember, courage is not recklessness. You're no good to anyone if you are killed or captured. Listen to your intuition and keep your wits about you. Sometimes it's braver to stop than to carry on.'

'Look after the umbrella for me.' Pip met the hedgehog's gaze with a soft smile, knowing the hedgehog would guard it fiercely.

Pie leaped into the air and swiftly flew past the ruined castle tower looming over the moonlit valley on the left and silently approached the thicket hiding the tanks from view. Pip easily spied their stark, angular bodies jutting out from beneath freshly felled branches placed over long gun barrels and steel hulls. As they neared, she tightly grasped the ring of beeswax hanging over her shoulder. Pie fanned out his tail feathers and landed with a clunk between the two grates covering both fuel compartments at the rear of the tank.

'Follow me,' Monique whispered, sliding from the magpie's back.

Pip shivered at the cold metal under her paws and bounded after the ermine, squeezing head first through the grate to their right. She hurried after Monique with the smell of petrol rushing up her nose. Quaking, she carefully lowered herself to the narrow upper ledge of the fuel tank and stared at a sheet-metal slope, steeply descending towards a wall covered with thin, horizontal bars.

'Whatever you do,' Monique said gravely, 'don't slip down there. It's almost impossible to climb back up and if the engine starts running you'll be fried by *that*.' Pip stared at the grille and felt her heart thump in her stomach.

'Watch and learn.' Monique scampered to the middle of the ledge where a cylinder stretched upwards with two long fuel lines protruding from either side. The ermine's long fangs glinted in the gloom, then she sank her teeth into the rubber wires with a thrash of her head. 'See?' She smiled, releasing her grip and pointing her paw at four damp punctures before quickly filling them with clumps of beeswax. 'It's easy!'

Feeling a surge of excitement, Pip did the same and spat out the bitter taste of petrol that seeped around her gums before she pressed beeswax into the holes.

'*Bon!*' Monique beamed. 'Now for the left side of the machine. I'll follow you this time.' The ermine linked her paws together and made a step for Pip to stand on. 'Climb up and I'll meet you out there.'

With a boost from Monique from below, Pip easily

pulled herself back into the night and locked eyes with Pie, staring down at her with his glossy black-and-white feathers shining in the light of the moon.

'Come on,' the ermine whispered, clambering out through the grate. 'This way!'

Racing past Pie, they hurried to the grate on the left side of the tank, slipped into the fuel compartment and swiftly sabotaged the fuel lines before reappearing in the gloom.

'One metal monster down, two to go,' the magpie whispered as Pip and Monique clambered on to his back again.

Pie headed for the next tank, parked a few metres away behind a screen of tangled branches and leaves. But as the magpie perched on the machine, Pip's nose twitched, smelling stale smoke, and her senses pricked, knowing danger lurked nearby.

'Something's burning,' Pip whispered, sniffing as she slid with Monique from Pie's back, darting her eyes around the clearing, slowly becoming brighter under the sinking moon.

'Cigarettes.' Pie shuddered, cocking his head in all directions searching for men. 'The soldiers must be in foxholes beneath this tank.' His feathers ruffled with unease around his neck. 'Move fast and listen out for my warning. If you hear my call, you must come out at once. Do you understand?'

The little mouse and the ermine looked at one another and nodded, and in a matter of minutes they had sabotaged the fuel lines. It was when Pip and Monique were clambering on to Pie's back again that they suddenly heard footsteps behind them. Holding their breaths, they watched a soldier sprint down the bank of the castle mound towards the tank they'd just left. Leaping upon it, he creaked open the hatch in its turret and slammed it closed behind him with a metallic thud.

'We're running out of time,' Pie said, beating his wings as fast as he could towards the third and final machine, overlooking a steep decline into the valley. 'That soldier has something on his mind.'

'Hurry, Pie!' Pip whispered, trying to ignore the feeling of dread knotting inside her. 'I know we can do this before they catch us!'

They landed on the last tank with a final clunk of the magpie's claws and Pip's heart pounded, hearing a severe German voice crackle on a radio inside.

'*Jawohl!*' a man barked inside. '*Heil Hitler!*'

'This tank has received some kind of order,' Pie said

urgently. 'We must stop it before it heads into battle.'

Pip and Monique dashed into the left fuel compartment, trembling as they punctured the fuel lines and plugged them with beeswax, now whittled to small rings around their paws.

'We've only got the right-hand side to damage now,' Monique panted, giving Pip another boost out of the grate. 'Quickly, let's finish this!'

But at that moment, the tank jolted to life with a roar that chilled their blood.

'Abort!' Pie cawed, skittering over to meet them as the chug of the engine vibrated beneath their paws.

'Come on, Pip!' Monique cried, leaping on the magpie's back. Seeing Pip hesitate, the ermine yanked her up to straddle the bird in front of her. But Pip's mind whirred as the magpie launched into the air and she frowned, feeling a rush of impulse rise inside her.

'No! We just have one more fuel line to sabotage.' Pip shook her head, determination hardening her jaw. 'We're so close! We can't give up now!'

Pip threw herself from the magpie. Dropping like a stone, she slammed against the tank's metal hull and rolled across its surface, scrabbling for something to hold. Her body tumbled over the side and her claws caught the head of a screw bolted into the rear exhaust panel. She pulled herself up, feeling hot air blow against her fur.

It was then that the haunting sound of Gabriel and Madeleine's howls moaned from the trees behind her. As she snapped her head up and searched for Henri's antlers in the first dusky blues of dawn, her body grew rigid with fear. The two tanks they had just damaged were thundering towards her. The branches used to conceal them were shuddering off their metal shells, revealing monstrous gun barrels pointing straight at her. Pip darted to the metal

grate over the final fuel compartment and hurried inside. The heat radiating from the grille was stifling as she feverishly ripped the fuel lines open with her teeth and pushed the last pieces of the beeswax into the holes. Triumphant, she gazed up at the grate over her head and her stomach lurched in dismay. Monique wasn't there to lift her out.

The tank lunged forward, and Pip, panic thrumming, felt her paws slipping from under her. At once the radiator grille tugged at her limbs, and Pip desperately leaped and clamped her claws into the fuel line. With relief surging through her, she followed the length of the cable to where it was pinned against the wall, and used it as a shelf to clamber into the open air.

The tank rattled and squeaked as it teetered over the edge of the clearing and into the valley below. Quaking, Pip looked down at the grass racing alongside her and hurled herself from the machine. A moment later, she somersaulted across the ground and found herself lying on her back, staring into the murky wisps of dawn clouds. The other two tanks rolled past her down the hill and Pip breathed a sigh laced with terror, glad to feel cool dewdrops soaking her fur.

'Pip!' Pie cried, swooping beside her. 'Are you all right?'

Monique raced from Pie's back. 'Are you hurt?' Pip turned her head to meet their gaze and a broad smile spread across her little face. They all laughed, their fears dissolving into exhilaration.

'Unbelievable!' Pie chuckled.

'Absolutely stupid!' Madame Fourcade corrected, scowling between Henri's ears as he and the wolves skidded to a halt beside them. The bats blinked inquisitively from their perch above the umbrella cradled across his antlers. 'What did I say about excessive daring?' the hedgehog continued as Henri lowered his head to the ground and Madame Fourcade hurried to Pip with bristling prickles. 'You could have been killed!'

'But I couldn't let it get away –' Pip wobbled to a stand, adrenalin still rippling under her fur – 'not when we were so close.'

'You had already sabotaged the fuel tank on one side,' Madame Fourcade scolded. 'That metal monster would've run out of petrol too, just a little later than the others.'

'But it could have driven further and got help,' Pip said defiantly.

'I thought I'd lost you.' The hedgehog threw her paws round Pip. 'You are not supposed to die until your fur has turned white and your own kittens have driven you mad with worry.'

Pip sank into Madame Fourcade's embrace. She didn't mind it when Madame Fourcade got angry. Since she had lost Mama and Papa, Madame was the closest thing to family she had and the hedgehog seemed to agree. She hadn't seen her hoglets for years and she never spoke of where they were hidden, but Pip knew they were always in the back of her mind, especially when she told Pip how much she reminded her of them.

'Look!' Monique grinned, pointing her paw into the valley where a belt of orange sunrise crept over the eastern horizon. 'Over there by that windmill!'

The three tanks were spaced out along the open road below with their back bonnets cranked open. Beside them, the enemy soldiers hopped up and down in rage, just as Monique had predicted.

'We did it!' Pip beamed. 'I can't wait to tell GI Joe!'

'Everyone is going to enjoy this story.' Gabriel's tongue hung out of his mouth in a smile. 'Another tale from the legends of the Umbrella Mouse will fill them with hope.'

CHAPTER NINE

THE MILICE

The animals left the ruined castle glowing in the first pinks and golds of sunrise and made their way back down the hill towards the Maquis's cavern, the bats circling in the air above their heads, vigilantly scanning the surrounding forest for any signs of the Rogue Wolves and the Butcher Birds.

The headiness of the sabotage was easing and a cheerful weariness clung to Pip and her friends. She looked forward to their return to the cavern, where they could share their story and catch up on the sleep they'd missed. Pip hoped that GI Joe was feeling better, and pictured his face lighting up when she told him about their victory over the Tiger tanks. But an uneasy feeling crept over her when she remembered Jude the canary suggesting GI Joe had been turned into an enemy spy. She hoped the successful sabotage would prove to Jude that he had nothing to fear.

They were nearing the Maquis's hideout when they froze, hearing something whimper ahead.

'Don't move,' Gabriel said gruffly.

The magpie on his back cocked his head with his eyes roving across the forest. Madeleine stepped forward with her hackles rising, but as they listened again they heard only the leaves rustling in the wind.

'It's nothing,' Madeleine whispered. 'Keep moving. We're not far from the cavern.'

The animals crept forward for a moment before freezing again. Ahead, a small bird hobbled out of the undergrowth and limped across the forest floor. Its open wings dragged at crooked angles across the ground and its feathers were a mottled orange colour Pip had not seen before. It collapsed on its side and Pie launched from Gabriel's back to get a closer look.

'Who are you?' the magpie asked softly, landing at a cautious distance near the bird. 'What happened to you?'

'Pie?' The bird lifted its head weakly in the direction of his voice and Pip gasped, realizing its eyes were hollow and the yellow feathers around its face were clumped with dried blood. 'Is that you?'

'*Jude?*' the magpie gasped. The other animals looked at

one another in alarm and rushed to the canary's side. 'Who did this to you?'

'The Butcher Birds.' Jude wept. 'And a white pigeon.'

'Lucia's alive?' Pip said, aghast.

'She will have been punished for her failure to stop our escape from the Nacht und Nebel camp,' Madame Fourcade said. 'We need to get away from here.'

'The Rogue Wolves are with them too,' Jude added, agony ruffling his feathers all over his body. 'Be careful. They will catch your scent.'

'Villains,' Madeleine growled. 'They have no heart, no reason – just murder and chaos.'

'How did they find you?' Monique the ermine interrupted, her voice trembling as she crouched beside the canary. 'Is the cavern safe?'

The canary was silent for a moment before his face crumpled with shame.

'I couldn't risk capture and stay with you when you were harbouring the Umbrella Mouse,' he moaned. Pip's breath caught in her throat. This was her fault. 'I left the cavern when Gaspard sent me to fetch water and honey from the bees . . .' His breath rasped weakly, and the animals shared glances of horror. They'd been so focused on discussing the sabotage of the Tiger tanks that none of them had realized

Jude hadn't returned with the bees before. 'Shortly after I escaped the brambles, the Butcher Birds and the pigeon caught sight of me. I tried to hide, but there were too many of them. I couldn't escape. I was surrounded and . . . and . . . I knew having the Umbrella Mouse with us was too dangerous!' he moaned bitterly. 'She's led us all to our doom. It's her fault! Not mine . . . I couldn't help it . . . the pain . . . I couldn't stop myself.'

'Stop what, Jude?' Madame Fourcade's prickles bristled.

Pip winced at the sight of him suffering so much. She couldn't tell which was worse for him, his injuries or what he was trying to say.

'What did you tell them, Jude?' Gabriel asked through gritted teeth.

'I only wanted to be safe,' the canary whispered raggedly. 'I never thought . . .'

The animals shuddered, watching Jude's body contort with pain. A moment later, the canary flopped forward with his head upon his broken wing. The air grew cold with death and the animals' ears pricked, hearing squeaks above their heads.

'Don't take another step!' the bats cried, returning and frantically circling their heads. 'The Rogue Wolves and the Butcher Birds have found our hideout!'

All the animals cowered, and one by one their eyes flicked to the canary lying at their paws.

'Jude betrayed us!' Pie the magpie said angrily, and Monique the ermine covered her face with her paws in despair. Hopping to her, Pie wrapped one of his wings round her shoulders. 'He abandoned us so he wouldn't risk capture.'

'And in doing so,' Madeleine growled, 'he's killed himself.'

'And others too.' The bats swirled about them in distress. 'The gatekeepers' bodies are slumped against the opening to the brambles.'

'What about GI Joe and the rest of the Maquis?' Pip asked, her insides thundering with fear. Madame Fourcade drew her close and her prickles quivered against Pip's fur. 'Could they have escaped?'

'We don't know,' the bats continued gravely. 'We saw three Rogue Wolves canter east into the forest. Two shrikes are keeping watch at the bramble gates. They cackled as the wolves left.'

'We have to do something!' Pip cried. 'We must go and see who's survived. We can't just leave them there. If they're alive, they need our help!'

'It's hopeless.' Monique the ermine looked up at Pip

with eyes that glistened with tears. 'If we go back, we'll be captured or killed too.'

'But we have no choice,' Madame Fourcade added with a desperate shake of her head. 'If Jude told the enemy about the cavern, we have to assume he told them everything he knew about Pip as well.' Her brow creased as her thoughts went to the hours before. 'I mentioned Paris and that we were travelling east! That means the Milice have a good idea of where we are headed and our onward journey is in peril.'

'And if anyone talked inside the cavern they'll know we left it to sabotage the tanks.' Pie cocked his head in the direction they'd just travelled. 'The Milice could be searching for us in the forest as we speak.'

'That means we're surrounded.' Henri shifted uneasily on his hooves.

'Then we must move quickly and stealthily.' Madame Fourcade's jaw hardened. 'We need to go to the brambles and find out what danger lies ahead, otherwise we could be walking straight into a trap. If we can, we'll go inside and see who has survived or escaped, then we need to find a safer hideout, and fast.'

'We can go to our old den to the north of Louviers,' Madeleine offered, Gabriel nodding beside her. 'It's half a day's journey from the brambles. We'll be safe there and we have friends nearby – a flock of seagulls – who deliver intelligence to the Resistance in Paris. They may be able to help you get there.'

'*Bon*,' Madame Fourcade said urgently. 'If we don't eat and rest soon, we'll become a danger to ourselves. Now, let's go!' She beckoned them forward with her paws. 'Go!'

CHAPTER TEN

THE BUTCHER BIRDS

The animals trod lightly as they crept behind the thickest ground ferns, hiding their advance towards the cavern. In the quiet, the softest breath seemed to be a bellow and Pip's heart clamoured in her ears so fiercely that she felt sure it would give them all away.

'The brambles are on the other side of this bank,' Madeleine whispered, stopping in her tracks, Gabriel beside her.

'Put me down, Henri,' Madame Fourcade ordered, and he lowered his head to the ground with the bats swinging from his antlers. Pip and Madame marched down the bridge of his long face and jumped from the end of his nose while Pie and Monique leaped from the wolves to join them on the ground. 'Gabriel, Madeleine and Henri –' the hedgehog pointed her paw to the undergrowth – 'take

83

cover under the thicket over there. Only small animals have a chance of going unseen from the crest of this hill.'

'Be careful,' Henri said softly. 'We'll keep watch the whole time.'

'Stay low.' Madame Fourcade glanced at his antlers. 'An umbrella in a forest is strange enough at the best of times.'

Pip gazed at it and felt a tug in her chest. The battered umbrella looked so normal in Henri's antlers now that she almost couldn't remember it sitting in pride of place in the shop window in London. It seemed unreal, as though her memories were a dream.

'Let's go.' Madeleine turned with Gabriel. Henri gave Pip an affectionate nudge of his nose before following the wolves, bent low so that his chin skimmed the forest floor.

'Follow me,' Madame Fourcade whispered to Pip, Monique and Pie, and they crept slowly up the bank, nerves jangling.

The forest swished above them and they slowed, allowing only their eyes to peek over the bank. Below, two grey birds with black masked heads sat either side of the entrance to the bramble maze. The shrikes were not big, larger than a sparrow yet smaller than a starling, and Pip breathed easier, finding them not nearly as threatening as she'd imagined. But then she saw what lay beside them. Impaled on the thorns, another bird with inky feathers and a white underbelly dangled, bloodied and torn. Its species was unrecognizable, and she and Madame Fourcade swallowed, seeing the shrikes' hooked beaks and talons.

'Listen,' Monique whispered, her ears snapping forward.

The clattering of wings was growing rapidly louder. A moment later they all instinctively ducked when a cloud of shrikes fluttered from beneath the brambles and swirled in the air above the two guards. Pip's throat pounded as a white pigeon with milky blue eyes dived through the throng and settled on the thorns.

'We've got everything we need,' Lucia cried, cocking her head to her army of Butcher Birds scattering themselves upon the brambles with their cold black gazes staring obediently. 'We've killed everyone inside and the Umbrella Mouse and Noah's Ark cannot be far ahead of us. We must trap her before her story travels any further. Spread out on the journey east toward Paris. Madame Fourcade is up to something,' she spat, as if saying the hedgehog's name left a bad taste in her mouth. 'Leave no stone unturned! I must have justice for Noah's Ark's escape from the camp! I want to watch Pip and Madame Fourcade blister and burn, just like that villainous eagle and that traitorous rat we picked out of the ashes!' Lucia shrieked. 'The myth of the mouse who undermined the regime must be destroyed!'

The Butcher Birds cheered with high-pitched screams, and a sickening wave of grief made Pip feel faint. Sinking her head into Madame Fourcade's embrace, her mind flashed with memories of Hans's and Léon's smiling faces, the warmth of their bodies and the kindness they'd shown when she'd lost everything she'd known.

'Terror will replace hope in the hearts of the Resistance!' Lucia continued. 'Interrogate and kill every member you find on sight. Punish their friends, crush their families and, at each stop you make on your way to Paris, tell every animal you see that we have wiped out the Maquis. No one will ever dare to rise up against us again! The hunt is on! The Resistance will think twice before helping a pitiful little mouse kitten once they know only pain and death will follow! We shall have our vengeance! Now *fly!*'

Pip and her friends ducked as the white pigeon and the swarm of shrikes whirled into the air and disappeared into the distant trees.

A chill descended on the brambles as the animals held their breaths and peered over the crest of the bank again, their ears alert for signs of the enemy. A few minutes passed and they exhaled, knowing they were alone.

'That vicious . . .' Madame Fourcade growled furiously, catching herself before she swore. She looked down at Pip, still clinging to her, and her face softened, meeting her devastated gaze. 'We will avenge Hans and Léon, and I will never let them touch you, *chérie*,' she vowed. Her voice was firm but her eyes glittered with tears. 'Lucia and the Milice's days are numbered. Our liberation will make sure of that. Henri, Gabriel, Madeleine,' she called, her voice still hushed. 'They've gone.'

'Come on,' Pip said defiantly, wiping the upset from her face with a shivering paw and bounding over the bank with a lump of sorrow in her throat. 'We have to see if anyone survived.'

'I'll take you,' Madeleine said, trotting after her with the white wolf, and bending her head to the ground. 'It will be quicker this way.'

Pip looked into the she-wolf's face with a quiver of unease. She'd never known a more frightening creature, and being this close to her made all her senses tingle with danger.

'There's no need to be afraid, little one.' Madeleine gave Pip a friendly nudge with her cold, wet nose, and when Pip met her gaze she could see the worry and sadness clouding the wolf's silver eyes.

Pip reminded herself that the wolves had done nothing but protect her. She clutched the grey wolf's coarse fur and clambered up to stand between her ears.

'Let's go,' Henri said, catching up, with Madame Fourcade on his head and the bats swinging from his antlers.

'Follow me,' Pie clacked, carrying Monique on his back.

They tried not to look at the remains of the gatekeepers as Pie led the way through the bramble maze with the others cantering behind. Weaving in and out of the barbed corridors through sheaths of light where the morning sunshine pierced the roof of thorns, they soon approached the opening to the cave, and slowed with their ears flattening against their heads. The beehive no longer hung above the opening. It lay in pieces across the forest floor, dotted with small grey feathers and the curled-up bodies of honeybees and bats, strewn across the ground. Seeing their fallen friends, the bats dangling from Henri's antlers yelped and covered their faces with their wings. Monique's lips trembled as Pie landed beside a bee and tenderly nudged its remains with his beak.

'This was a massacre.' Madame Fourcade shook her head in despair with Henri. It was the most horrible thing Pip had ever seen and she looked away, knowing the sight would haunt her forever.

The air grew heavy with dread as the animals followed Pie into the cave, which glowed dimly in the light of the bioluminescent mushrooms growing up the walls. The large cavern inside was cold and black without the glitter of the fireflies and a metallic, musky smell made Pip's blood thunder in her ears.

Madeleine sniffed with Gabriel, their hackles rising with the others' as they arrived. 'The Rogue Wolves were here . . .'

'Gaspard!' Pip cried, spotting a large shape slumped on the ground in the gloom beneath a cluster of mushrooms, lighting up a crown of antlers laced with webs of silk.

'The Great Stag.' Henri's voice cracked, stepping forward with a shuddering rump, and Pip gasped, knowing Gaspard was dead. A stab of guilt throbbed in her gut. Lucia had killed him and the others to get to her.

'I can't bear it!' Monique whimpered, burying her head in Pie's feathers.

'Amélie's not in his horns!' Pip cried, her chest pounding as she pointed her paw into the spider webs draped across his antlers. 'The fireflies aren't here either,' she added, craning her neck up to the ceiling of roots where they had dangled over the cavern. 'Where's GI Joe?' Pip whipped round urgently. 'We left him right here with Amélie and the others. Could the enemy have taken them all?'

'The wolves and the shrikes had no prisoners with them,' the bats squeaked from Henri's antlers.

'Then maybe they escaped?' Pip desperately searched for a place where they could have fled, but there was nowhere she could see.

The other animals caught one another's gazes and their faces fell with the same macabre thought.

CHAPTER ELEVEN

DEARLY DEPARTED

'I know what you're thinking . . .' Pip's voice faltered. 'But if the Rogue Wolves and the Butcher Birds *had* eaten them, wouldn't there be feathers or fireflies on the ground?' She squinted in the gloom at the dark earthen floor. 'And look! There aren't any! Maybe they escaped to where the sphagnum moss is, we can't just—'

'Pip?' a voice suddenly uttered above their heads, making them all jump. A yellow-green dot flashed on the ceiling, followed by one after another until the dark chamber twinkled with the glow of fireflies, lighting up hiding places behind the tree roots encasing the walls and ceiling.

'Amélie!' Pip cried, watching the spider sink to the ground by a long thread of silk. She landed with her eight legs crumpling. Pip hurried down Madeleine's fur to meet her. 'Are you all right?' She scanned the cavern again. 'Where's GI Joe?'

'He's hidden up there,' Amélie said, weakly pointing her tarsus to the wooden tendrils sprawled over their heads. 'I used all the strength I had to conceal his cocoon within them. The fireflies covered my web with earth they collected from the ground and camouflaged him.'

'I'll help them bring him down.' Pie leaped into the air from Gabriel's back and fluttered with difficulty around a mound densely woven into the tree roots above. Darting in and out, he slowly pecked around it, his beak gathering clumps of silk as the fireflies hovered nearby.

'Amélie.' Pip took one of her tarsi in her paw and gazed into the spider's ashen face, not knowing what to do. Behind her, Henri lowered his head to the ground and the hedgehog hurried from his nose to join them.

'Thank goodness you're safe,' Amélie said. 'We were so worried they would find you.'

'What happened?' Madame Fourcade asked, crouching beside the spider with a furrowed brow.

'We were sleeping when we were ambushed.' Amélie's eight eyes glistened with tears. 'The bees must have been overwhelmed – we woke to shrill cries echoing all through the cavern.' The spider sniffed as she met the hedgehog's gaze. 'We've always been so careful that we thought we'd never be found, but there were too many of them. We didn't stand a chance.'

'What happened to Gaspard?' Madeleine whimpered, lying flat on her stomach with Gabriel, who was resting his chin sorrowfully between his paws.

'When we heard the commotion,' Amélie went on, 'Gaspard ordered me and the fireflies to take GI Joe with the bats and escape. The bats fled and we feared the worst when we heard screaming intensify outside. GI Joe was too heavy for us to carry with any speed so the fireflies flew us to the ceiling where we all took refuge behind the roots. Then the Rogue Wolves and the Butcher Birds arrived with a white pigeon and they interrogated Gaspard.' Amélie wept. 'The pigeon was so cruel to him.'

The hedgehog frowned. 'Did Gaspard tell them about us?'

'No, he tried to convince them we were not the Resistance.' Amélie sniffed. 'He pretended that he wanted to help the enemy, but our canary Jude had told them everything. Gaspard lied, saying Jude couldn't be trusted and he'd heard that the Umbrella Mouse had already reached Paris. But the white pigeon didn't believe him. She ordered the wolves to kill him and she told them to hunt Noah's Ark on their journey to Paris.' Amélie took a long, shuddering breath and her voice grew heavy with anger. 'How could Jude do this to us? What will I do without Gaspard?' She wept. 'I've spent my whole life living in his horns.'

'I wish we'd never come to you.' Madame Fourcade's eyes glistened with tears as she hung her head in remorse. 'You came to our aid and we brought the disaster you feared.'

'This happened because of me.' Pip trembled, fear and fury rising inside her. 'Lucia and the Milice are punishing everyone for what I did to her at the Nacht und Nebel camp. If it wasn't for me, none of this would have happened!'

'No, we don't blame you.' Amélie shook her head sorrowfully with the rest of the Maquis. 'It's not just you they are hunting. They want revenge against the whole Resistance for helping the Allies.'

'Lucia and the enemy could have done us much more damage if you had not helped us in the way that you did, Pip,' Madame Fourcade said softly. 'The only way we can stop Lucia and the Milice is to liberate France. Paris will be a victory the enemy cannot ignore and the Allies will push the invaders back to Berlin where they belong. We're so close to the end,' she continued, looking up at the grief-stricken animals inside the cavern. 'The time has come to unite. I know you have worked alone until now, but our betrayal, hurt and anger can be harnessed for the oncoming fight.'

'Amélie.' Pip stared earnestly at the spider. 'Why don't you and the Maquis join Noah's Ark and come with us? We're all fighting the same cause and together we'll be stronger.'

'We'd be honoured to have you,' Madame Fourcade added. 'The more fighters we have, the sooner we'll beat the invaders and end this loathsome war. The rest of our group are waiting for us in the catacombs.'

'Gaspard wanted freedom above all else,' Amélie said sadly in the green-lit gloom, looking up at the remaining members of the Maquis. 'The only way we can protect his forest for good is by joining the wider fight and avenging our friends.'

'But we'll need to split into two groups,' Madame Fourcade added as the other animals nodded softly in agreement. 'It'll be safer for us all.'

'There are so few of the Maquis left,' Pie said, finally detaching GI Joe from the ceiling and gliding to Amélie's side. 'The bats and I can take Monique, Amélie and the fireflies, and we'll meet the rest of you in Paris.'

'And we'll come with you as far as we can, Madame,' Gabriel added, 'but we cannot go near a city. The humans fear wolves too much. We will stay in the forest and make sure there are no counter-attacks to the Allied advance from the west, just like Gaspard wanted. Madeleine and I will travel with you and protect Henri once we can go no further.'

'And then I will fight alongside you.' The stag turned to the wolves, who were gently wagging their tails in approval, and Pip felt better, knowing Henri would be safer with them than on his own.

'Why didn't you let me outta this damn bandage and let me fight?' GI Joe interrupted, floating to the ground on a bed of fireflies, and still tightly wrapped inside his cocoon.

'You'd have been too weak,' Amélie said wearily. 'We promised we would take care of you while your friends were gone.'

'Being inside this is a prison!' GI Joe cried. 'I owe you my life, Amélie and all, and for that I'm truly grateful, but seeing Lucia again . . . and watching her . . .' He closed his eyes and tried to shake the memory from his head. 'I felt so helpless! Madame Fourcade, please, I'm begging you. I've had all the honey, rest and medicine I can stand! You gotta let me out now!'

'You certainly sound more like yourself,' the hedgehog said, glancing at Amélie and the fireflies. The insects nodded softly one after another, too fatigued with grief to argue.

'Monique,' Amélie said to the ermine, 'your teeth will free him the fastest.'

'I'll help,' Pip said, moving over to him.

'How you doin', liddle lady?' GI Joe gazed fondly at her. She smiled sadly in reply and bit her lip, trying her hardest not to cry.

GI Joe's cocoon was crisp and dry as though he'd been baked inside a stale loaf of bread. With a crunch of their teeth, Monique and Pip prised it away piece by piece, spitting out earthy sphagnum moss as they went. Together they made a large hole over GI Joe's chest and when Pip could see his feathers beneath she feverishly snapped off bigger chunks with her paws.

'That's it!' GI Joe smiled, wiggling his shoulders and flexing his pink talons in the open air, until at last he burst open his wings and rolled himself on to his stomach. He wobbled to a stand and swayed from side to side. Pip threw herself into his body and supported his weight with her own.

'Let's go get these maggots!' GI Joe cooed, puffing out his chest, and Pip staggered as he lost his balance.

'We'll leave as soon as possible, but you are in no fit

state to fight, *mon ami*.' Madame Fourcade raised her paw as he opened his beak to protest. Recognizing the stubborn expression scored across her face, he promptly closed it. 'That's my final word. You won't be any use until you've recovered.'

'We will all need time to heal from this blow, especially the Maquis,' Henri said. 'We must sleep and eat and regather our strength.'

Pip looked at the animals, drooping with exhaustion in the chamber. The weight of the last hours made her feel dizzy and heavy all at once, and her mind whirred with everything that had happened. Sleeping wouldn't be easy.

'It's time for us to split up and get out of this tomb,' Gabriel said. 'We'll take Pip, Madame Fourcade, Henri and GI Joe to our old den where we'll be safe to rest. It's half a day's journey east towards Paris. If we leave now, we'll arrive before sunset, then we'll take you to the seagulls tomorrow morning. Hopefully they can help you get into the city.'

Madame Fourcade nodded. 'Then let's depart. The longer we wait, the weaker our wits, and we'll need them intact if we cross paths with the enemy. Everyone: keep your eyes and ears open on the onward journey. They'll be circling the route to Paris, waiting for us to make a mistake.'

*

Henri trod into the forest with Pip, Madame Fourcade and GI Joe nestled together on his head, the umbrella carried across his antlers and the wolves flanking him on either side, often raising and dipping their noses for any scent from the Rogue Wolves.

'*Au revoir!*' Monique and Amélie waved, straddled across Pie, who was flying overhead beside the two bats, and all of them had fireflies clinging to their bodies. '*À bientôt à Paris!*'

Pip waved back, her chest tightening. 'Will they be all right?'

'Let's hope so,' Madame Fourcade said comfortingly, 'and we'll get sick with worry if we listen to our fears. We must think of the happiness we'll feel when we're reunited, not what trouble we may find ahead.'

'Come.' Gabriel picked up pace with Madeleine. 'Our den is north of Louviers along the banks of the River Seine.'

'*C'est bon.*' Madame Fourcade smiled softly as Henri cantered beside the wolves. 'We can follow the river, it flows right through the middle of the city, and once we're there we'll soon find the white mouse.'

'How do you know her?' Pip asked.

'We've never met,' Madame Fourcade said, 'but we

have communicated by Morse code a number of times. She is famous among the Resistance – she's a New Zealander who settled in Australia and she's been in Europe for years. Her love for France and her hatred for the enemy is well known. She's a spirited fighter and her network has been readying the animal Resistance for an uprising for some time now. They'll welcome us, you'll see, and we'll battle for our freedom together with the rest of Noah's Ark. You will adore Paris, *chérie*. The enemy has sullied it with its soldiers and flags, but the city's beauty still reigns. It did not suffer a Blitz, like London. Britain is protected by water, whereas we border Germany. We were overwhelmed by the invaders and forced to capitulate. You'll see that Paris is remarkably unchanged.'

London will always be my favourite city, though, Pip thought, remembering the red buses, the telephone boxes, the people coming into the umbrella shop to grumble about the weather, and the men and women walking arm in arm as they looked at the umbrellas in the window on their way to the theatre. Seeing Mama and Papa in her memory, she swallowed a lump in her throat, finding their faces too hard to bear.

'Just you wait until you see the Eiffel Tower.' GI Joe

winked, noticing her whiskers drooping on her cheeks. 'There's nothing like it.'

For the rest of the day, the stag and the wolves continued east, travelling as quickly and quietly as they could through the forest and taking cover whenever they heard an unexpected sound or saw a flutter in the undergrowth they did not like.

It was a slow journey, and the August sun had scorched the sky red when they reached the den near the river, which rippled like molten gold against the fading light. Gabriel and Madeleine led the way, bounding along the bank before swerving to the right and abruptly disappearing under the treeline, bringing the animals to a grassy ditch with a large, earthy hole burrowed into the ground.

'It's deep enough so we won't be seen or heard.' Madeleine sniffed the entrance to the den she'd dug some time ago. 'And it will keep us dry if the weather turns.'

'*Parfait*.' Madame Fourcade smiled. 'I can think of no better place for us to gather our strength.'

'But Henri won't fit inside.' Pip's brow furrowed. 'We can't stay here if he's going to be in danger.'

'She's right,' GI Joe added. 'It's your antlers, buddy.'

'I'll be fine if I lie down and keep my head low,' Henri

said calmly, stepping into the ditch and tucking his legs under him.

'We'll stay close and keep watch,' Madeleine said. 'I promise he'll come to no harm. We build our dens in the safest places so our cubs are not at risk.' Suddenly Madeleine's eyes clouded and Gabriel nuzzled his head into her neck. 'If we had stayed here with ours,' she said, blinking away tears, 'the Rogue Wolves would never have killed them.'

Pip hadn't considered Madeleine being a mother. Both she and Gabriel were young and fierce; it made sense for them to have cubs and, as she looked at the wolves comforting each another, she sighed, realizing grief haunted even the most powerful creatures.

'No words can make up for your loss,' Madame Fourcade said warmly, 'but you will always be a mother, no matter what happened to your young.'

Looking up from Gabriel's fur, Madeleine met the hedgehog's gaze.

'It feels good to be here again.' Madeleine smiled softly. 'It's full of happy memories.'

Gabriel's gold eyes shone. 'And one day I hope it will be filled with many more.'

'Now,' Madame Fourcade said, sympathetically

changing the subject, 'we've had a long and perilous journey, so we must eat!' Pip's stomach gurgled and the hedgehog laughed beside her. 'Your belly sounds as empty as mine!'

Beneath the first shimmer of stars, Pip and Madame Fourcade snuffled in the undergrowth above the wolves' den and nibbled on freshly foraged blackberries, acorns and seeds, while GI Joe exercised his weakened wings and flew unsteadily between low-hanging branches above their heads.

When Pip was finally full, she wiped the juice from her lips and sat heavily with her legs stretched out before her, watching the stag's silhouette graze the grass along the moon-drenched riverbank. Behind him, Gabriel and Madeleine waded into the river. One after another, they darted their muzzles through the surface and reappeared with large fish wriggling between their teeth. Leaping triumphantly out of the river, they trotted to dry land and feasted on their catches with swishing tails. It was a scene as normal for woodland animals as any Pip could imagine, and for a brief moment she forgot the world was at war.

Fed and watered, the animals retired, with Henri and the wolves curling up in the grassy ditch, and Pip, Madame Fourcade and GI Joe nestling together inside

the den, which was bare except for a scattering of dried leaves and the warm smell of family. Pip snuggled against the hedgehog's soft belly fur and felt comforted by her friends' gentle snores. Slowly, her eyes grew heavier and she slumped into a deep, worn-out sleep.

CHAPTER TWELVE

HOPE

Pip woke with a start, seeing Léon and Hans's final struggle against the sentry owls and Goliath Rats at the Nacht und Nebel camp twist painfully in her mind. Trembling from the tips of her whiskers to the end of her tail, her gaze slowly came into focus and she breathed easier, finding Madame Fourcade and GI Joe peacefully sleeping beside her in the wolf den. Feeling too shaken to close her eyes again, she sat upright with her knees pulled into her chest and cried as quietly as she could.

'Pip?' Madame Fourcade groggily moved over to her and wrapped her paws round her shuddering shoulders. 'What's wrong?'

'I should have done something to save Léon and Hans that night,' Pip sniffed, tears streaming down her face. 'Then they'd still be with us.'

'There's nothing you could'a done.' GI Joe cooed sleepily, untucking his head from under his wing and shuffling over to her. 'This damn war's to blame, not you.'

'He's right, *chérie*,' Madame Fourcade soothed. 'No matter how many "should"s and "could"s we utter, we cannot change what is done. Keep your head above water by remembering our friends in happier times. Reliving their last moments will only weigh you down.' Madame Fourcade paused, squeezing Pip tighter and resting her chin on the top of her head. 'I ache inside, thinking of you and my hoglets growing up in these terrible days of war. I cannot wait to introduce you to them after our liberation; they are not far from Paris at all. You have already been through so much for one so young. We will triumph, Pip, you'll see. Hope is a very powerful thing. Anything is possible if you can keep it burning, and the bravery you showed when you freed us from the Nacht und Nebel camp has lit the fires inside the hearts of the Resistance – and that's what scares the enemy the most.' The hedgehog's eyes twinkled with kindness. 'Do you know what always makes me feel better after a nightmare?' Pip shook her head. 'A bath.'

GI Joe nodded. 'Oh boy, that sounds good.'

'Let's wash away the horridness,' the hedgehog said, padding towards the entrance to the den, which was now lightening with the smoky blues of sunrise. 'It works wonders – you'll see.'

Pip, Madame Fourcade and GI Joe crawled into the open air, past Henri, still cradling the umbrella in his horns as he slept beside Madeleine and Gabriel in the ditch, and walked to the river, which mirrored the murky clouds ambling slowly across the sky. Reaching the water's edge, GI Joe waded up to his stomach and tossed his body from side to side and Pip mimicked Madame Fourcade, cupping her paws into the river and splashing her face with a gasp at the chill.

The cicadas woke, chirping their early morning melodies, and the water stilled. Pip's heart quickened, seeing her reflection for the first time in months. She had lost some of her fluffy fur and she could see she looked more like Mama now.

She felt the familiar press of Henri's nose gently nudge her shoulder. He padded into the shallows with the wolves and lowered his mouth to drink.

'If we find the seagulls soon,' Madeleine said, lifting her head to the sky, now bleeding pink and mauve, 'you could be in Paris by nightfall.'

Gabriel and Henri followed her gaze with water

dripping from their muzzles.

'I'm ready,' Pip said, with Madame Fourcade and GI Joe nodding beside her.

Henri smiled. 'Then climb back up, you three.'

Pip and Madame Fourcade scaled the length of his face to stand between his ears, but GI Joe shuffled on his talons, unsure of how to join them.

'Use your wings!' Pip offered, and GI Joe's brow furrowed in reply.

'I don't know, liddle lady.' He shook his head sadly. 'My aim isn't what it used to be. But here goes.'

With a frown of concentration, he bent his knees and leaned his body forward. Throwing up his wings and tail feathers and swiftly pulling them down again, he lifted himself into the air and landed unsteadily on Henri's face. The stag lifted his head and at once GI Joe stumbled and landed on his stomach with his wings wrapped around Henri's nose. They stared at each other, wide-eyed with alarm, before the pigeon cleared his throat with embarrassment and waddled to the crown of Henri's head.

'Worry not, *mon ami*,' Madame Fourcade said as GI Joe settled beside Henri's right antler with a doleful sigh. 'We may be better rested, but no one expects you to bounce back overnight after everything you have been through.'

'Ready?' Madeleine wagged her tail with Gabriel. 'Follow us!'

For the rest of the morning, Henri and the wolves cantered under the cover of trees and long grasses growing beside the river, winding through the forest. The shore grew woodier the further they travelled, and the animals slowed through tall shrubs and leafy boughs until they reached a place where the thicket abruptly thinned into thick green hedgerows and pastures, rolling into the horizon.

'Without the trees you can see for miles,' Gabriel whispered, his gold eyes scanning the countryside for danger.

'What's that noise?' Pip asked, ears pricking, hearing a low rumble grow rapidly louder overhead, and the animals halted, their necks craning into the clouds.

'Hide!' Madame Fourcade gasped as the noise rose to a pounding roar. The air shuddered as the animals leaped into the undergrowth and cowered, watching countless grey propeller planes pepper the blue above.

'Those are US bombers,' GI Joe cooed, watching them thunder into the countryside, and Pip breathed easier, hearing the river flow again. 'You can tell from the stars under the wings. And that's a whole lotta planes. We don't wanna be anywhere near them when they carry out their objective, believe me.'

'We should hurry.' Madeleine trotted ahead. 'The seagulls will be leaving for Paris to report them soon.'

'Off to inform the Jerries about those planes, are we?' came a gruff voice suddenly from the thicket. Henri shied backwards as an Alsatian with a white chest stepped out from behind a shrub with his nose wrinkling in a snarl. Madeleine and Gabriel growled and stalked forward, curling their lips back from their fangs.

'Who are you?' Pip's ears pricked at his English accent and her mind raced, seeing the harness wrapped around his body. It had a small bag attached, stitched with a red cross on the side, and Pip's heart swelled, remembering Dickin the London search and rescue dog's kind, scruffy face. Not only had he helped her during the most difficult time in her life, he had never tired of trying to make her smile. He was her first true friend.

'I think it's best you tell us who *you* are,' another Alsatian snapped from behind them. 'We have a battalion of men ready to attack at our call.'

'I dare you to do it,' Madeleine the she-wolf spat, 'but it'll be the last thing you ever do.'

'Stop it!' Pip cried as they circled one another. 'Don't you see? You're on the same side! You've come from

England, haven't you?' she asked the Alsatians. They stopped growling and Pip spoke as fast as she could. 'I knew a dog like you in London. His name was Dickin and he helped humans after bombing raids. He saved me when the umbrella shop where I lived was destroyed and my parents were killed. The wolves you are quarrelling with are members of the French Resistance, so *stop* fighting, all of you!'

'Is that so?' the first Alsatian asked, cocking his head at Pip standing between Henri's ears beneath the umbrella cradled across his antlers. 'I say!' He suddenly beamed, his tongue hanging out of his mouth in a smile. 'Are you Pip?'

'Yes,' she answered, sharing an astonished glance with her friends.

'I don't believe it!' The other Alsatian wagged his tail energetically and bounced over to Henri, who took two cautious steps backwards. 'What are the chances of us bumping into you like this? I'm Brian and we're members of Churchill's Secret Animal Army too! We've had special instructions via Bernard Booth's pigeon service to look out for you!'

'It's a pleasure to meet you fellows, I'm Bing,' the first Alsatian said, sitting on his haunches. 'Forgive us – we didn't mean to startle you. You're deep behind enemy lines and none of us can be too careful. We're sky-dogs and we're the eyes, ears and noses of our men.'

'Of course!' GI Joe cooed excitedly. 'You guys parachute with the boys and protect them on the ground, sniffing out mines and listening for the enemy, and you also deliver messages and medical supplies on the battlefield. I remember seeing three of you on the airfield before I boarded my paratroopers' plane for D-Day. Bernard Booth told us all about you.'

'Yes, he said about five hundred pigeons were joining us on the jump that night.' Brian smiled and GI Joe nodded proudly. 'We've communicated with a number of you since we arrived in France.'

'What are you doing here?' Pip asked, excited. She couldn't imagine dogs jumping out of planes with men during battles.

'The Allied army is pressing east through Normandy, but the enemy is fiercely counter-attacking around Falaise. We're here so our men can sabotage their electricity lines and demolish nearby bridges from inside enemy territory and delay their supply of food, fuel and weapons.'

'Have you seen the Jerries at all?' Bing asked. 'They use these blasted hedgerows for ambushing our men.'

'There were three Tiger tanks not far from here the night before last,' Pip said, 'but we sabotaged the fuel lines and stopped them in their tracks.'

'Well done!' Bing wagged his tail with Brian. 'I bet they didn't see that coming.'

'We must return to our troops soon.' Bing's ears cocked towards the brush. 'Bernard Booth gave us strict instructions to help you and any other Resistance network we come across – is there anything we can do for you?'

'Will you and your men come to Paris and help us liberate the city?' Pip pleaded, and her friends nodded around her.

'The Resistance is gathering strength,' Madame

Fourcade added. 'It's only a matter of time before they strike and, with military support, the invaders won't stand a chance against the civilian uprising.'

'We can't guarantee that, Madame.' Bing shook his head softly. 'If our operation is victorious, then our boys might be able to travel through Paris on our way to Berlin, but it's possible the Allies will bypass the city. They won't want to risk civilian lives or slow the advance towards Germany, especially as our fuel and food supplies are low. Brian and I must follow our orders and help our men put an end to all this mess.'

'We are meeting our contacts further down the river,' Gabriel said. 'We'd appreciate it if you made sure your men don't head in our direction.'

Brian nodded. 'You have our word. Anything else we can do for you now?'

'Have you seen any Butcher Birds?' Pip asked, and the Alsatians glanced at one another uneasily. 'They're small grey shrikes with black markings over their eyes like masks.'

Brian nodded again. 'We saw a mass of them heading east at dawn.' Pip's pulse raced. If they had left the wolf den any earlier, they could have crossed paths. 'It was strange,' Brian continued. 'All the sounds in the forest stopped, and, as we signalled for our boys to take cover, a sudden swarm of them passed overhead.'

'Beware,' Madeleine said gravely, 'they are members of the Milice – the French Resistance hunters.'

'They're searching for me.' Pip hung her head.

'They're afraid of you because they are losing the war,' Henri reassured her.

'The war isn't over yet.' Bing sighed. 'We still need to be vigilant every step of the way if we're going to be victorious, so take care on your onward journey.'

'Best of luck to you all.' Brian and Bing grinned with their tongues hanging out of their mouths.

Pip and the others smiled and wished them well. 'I hope we'll see you again.'

With that, the Alsatians leaped into the undergrowth and disappeared in a flurry of leaves.

'We just met sky-dogs!' GI Joe gave Pip an excited little nudge with his wing. 'Those guys are at the highest level an animal can get. With their help, the Allied army will make serious headway – no human can match a dog's hearing or sense of smell.'

Pip remembered how amazing Dickin was at finding people under the rubble. The humans wouldn't have known where to start without him, and if dogs could help the soldiers in battle too, there must be hope.

The roasting midday sun had already crested the sky when Pip and her friends neared a cluster of willows, which draped their long tendrils into the river. Panting in the heat, Henri and the wolves moved sluggishly towards the trees with Pip, Madame Fourcade and GI Joe drooping upon the stag's head. Madeleine led the way and parted the fine branches with the end of her nose, bringing them inside a cool, shady chamber enveloped by a canopy of fine, leafy branches swaying gently in the breeze.

At once, a cacophony of trumpeting screeches struck them as a large flock of herring gulls stood tall and glared at the new arrivals with pale, stony irises ringed with orange.

'*Silence!*' the biggest one cawed. The birds snapped their beaks shut and their snowy heads darted curiously from side to side. 'It's only Madeleine and Gabriel!' He turned to the wolves. 'What are these animals doing with you?'

The troop of gulls encircled the stag. Some bolder birds took flight and swooped about his head to get a closer look, and Henri, Pip and Madame Fourcade flinched in alarm as a gust of wings blasted their whiskers.

'Jeez!' GI Joe ducked and ruffled his neck feathers. 'You guys are friendly.'

'Stop!' Pip pleaded, stepping forward and protecting her eyes with an open paw raised to her brow. 'We need to get to Paris. Gabriel told us your colony delivers intelligence to the Resistance in the city. Please, we need your help.'

The seagull glared at the white wolf with a furious, stony stare.

'Relax, Claude,' Madeleine said calmly. 'We told them because we trust Pip and her friends, and so can you.'

Together, Madeleine, Pip and Madame Fourcade recounted the days and events that had brought them to the willow tree and soon the seagulls *yeow*ed excitedly, listening to Pip's story and the plan for the animal's onward quest.

'We've heard of you,' Claude remarked, 'but I thought you were a myth, teaching the Resistance that even the smallest creatures can make a big difference.' Pip shifted awkwardly on her paws. His cold, pale gaze made her insides turn. 'We know Paris and the Resistance groups operating within it very well. Our scouts are due back soon, then we'll report their findings to you. If it's safe to enter Paris, we can carry you, your umbrella, the hedgehog and that skinny pigeon too if you wish.'

'Thank you –' Pip breathed easier – 'but we need to tell you something.' She swallowed, seeing Gaspard and the

Maquis flash inside her mind. The gulls stared up at her and a few *kek-kek*ed, with their white heads darting from side to side. 'A white pigeon and an army of Butcher Birds are not far from here. They know we are heading to Paris and they'll interrogate and kill anyone who stands in their way.'

A ripple of laughter spread through the gulls. Pip frowned. She hadn't met anyone who didn't fear the Butcher Birds.

'We're not afraid of those little *crétins*.' Claude chuckled gleefully. 'They found us this morning, and, *oui*, they were looking for you.'

He turned his head to where the fine branches of the willow tree skimmed the grassy riverbank outside. Beneath the veil of leaves, Pip's eyes fell on clusters of grey feathers beyond the canopy and she gasped, realizing that small, grey bodies were scattered across the ground.

'We taught them a lesson they'll never forget,' Claude said bluntly. 'Those that survived won't dare come near us again. Twenty of us will travel to Paris this time, then they'll be the ones who are fleeing, not you.'

'What about the white pigeon?' Pip squeaked, seeing no white feathers or any bodies that were big enough to be Lucia's.

'That coward?' Claude scoffed. 'She bolted when we attacked.'

'If Lucia is scared of the gulls, then they will be the perfect bodyguards for us, *chérie*,' Madame Fourcade whispered in Pip's ear. Pip swallowed, not feeling so sure.

'Paris is vast and has many Resistance networks,' Claude went on. 'Who is your contact?'

'The white mouse,' Madame Fourcade answered.

'You mean Nancy!' he chortled. 'She's a funny one. She's organizing the different Resistance groups into an army with the stray cats and dogs in the city. The coypus, rats and ravens are also helping. We've known them since the beginning.'

'Coypus?' Pip's face scrunched up, wondering what the word meant.

'They have bodies like beavers,' Madame Fourcade said, 'and tails like rats – so a beaver-rat, if you will.'

Pip put the two together in her mind and felt a rush of desire to meet one.

'Their hideout is beside Colonel Rol's bunker – a human leader of the Paris Resistance,' Claude continued, enjoying Pip's excited expression, and puffing out his chest proudly. 'They've harnessed his electricity and they also secretly listen into Colonel Rol's progress so the animals can help the uprising in the most effective way.'

'*Génial!*' Madame Fourcade smiled. 'We've been instructed to find her in the catacombs via a hidden entrance in the Luxembourg Gardens.'

'There are many covert doors into the catacombs, Madame,' Claude interrupted, 'and we do not use that one for delivering intelligence. There is a swifter route we take by way of an abandoned railway track called La Petite Ceinture, but it's dangerous. If I take you, you must abide by my rules.'

A sudden clatter of wings sounded outside, and Pip and her friends flinched as three gulls torpedoed through the willow branches and landed among the colony. The birds jumped into the air with shrieks of surprise, and Pip covered her ears against the din.

'Good news!' one of the new arrivals cawed, her chest heaving up and down from the effort of fast flying. 'The human Allied army has encircled the enemy around the Falaise Pocket and forced thousands to surrender! The Allies are travelling east towards Paris and there's a real chance they can deliver the military aid we have been waiting for! The Resistance in Paris can rise!'

The animals inside the willow canopy roared with excitement. Madame Fourcade wrapped Pip in her arms

and squeezed her tightly while GI Joe enveloped them both with his wings. Madeleine and Gabriel nuzzled one another with wagging tails and Henri hopped on his hooves with joy.

'Say goodbye to the wolves and the stag,' Claude said brusquely before turning and pointing his wing into the crowd of birds, selecting twenty, twitching their wings in readiness to fly to Paris.

Pip's breath caught in her throat. How could she say goodbye to Henri after everything they had been through?

'Hurry up!' Claude waggled his tail impatiently, seeing Pip hesitate. 'We need to deliver our news! We see better in daylight. Our flight is safer before the moon rises.'

'It's time.' Henri lowered his head.

Madame Fourcade padded down his face to hop on to the grass and GI Joe leaped with a flap of his wings and landed clumsily on the ground beside her.

'We must go, *chérie*.' The hedgehog smiled sadly at Pip, who sat wretchedly between Henri's ears. She had made a

121

promise to help Noah's Ark end the war that had taken so much from them all. Only then could she make her final journey to Italy to find her mother's family in the umbrella museum.

Clambering down the bridge of Henri's nose, she reached the grass and threw her paws round his snout, trying to think of the words to tell him how much he meant to her, and she wept, finding none.

'I don't know how to say goodbye to you,' she sniffed.

'So let's not say it.' Henri's mahogany eyes gleamed. 'After all, who knows how soon we may see each other again? At times like these, we should say *bon courage*.'

'*Bon courage*, Henri,' she whispered, hugging him tighter.

'Besides, goodbyes don't mean the end,' Henri continued softly, 'they mean the start of something new.'

Pip released him from her embrace and traced the curve of his nose with her paw. She never wanted to forget his face, the texture of his fur and his head of antlers where he had carried her and her umbrella so many times.

'Hurry up!' Claude squawked, beating his wings with irritation.

'It's up to fate to bring us together again.' Madeleine briskly pressed her head against Pip's. 'We'll keep Henri safe.'

'Goodbye, little one,' Gabriel added, giving Pip a small lick with his tongue.

'We are still Noah's Ark even if we are not together –' Madame Fourcade wrapped her paw round Pip's shoulder – 'and the war is not won until the enemy is stopped, so *bon courage, mes amis*, and fight hard. I have faith that we will meet again.'

Pip, Madame Fourcade and GI Joe mounted the gulls, and as the birds launched into the air through the veil of fine willow branches. Pip looked over her shoulder for one last glimpse of Henri, and her heart swelled, seeing him rear up on to his hind legs to bid them farewell.

CHAPTER THIRTEEN

TO PARIS

Pip squinted in the bright afternoon sunshine as the seagulls soared over tall hedgerows and fields, unfurling into the distance like a gargantuan patchwork quilt below. She and Madame Fourcade straddled the back of a gull flying beside another carrying GI Joe. Both clasped the umbrella between their beaks, and together they charged through the sky in the middle of the flock of birds.

For what felt like an age, the birds swiftly followed the silver line of the river over woods, farmlands, tiny islands and small bridges, stretching over the water between villages and towns far below. Pip couldn't prise her eyes

from the view, and eagerly leaned her head over the side to watch the world go by with Madame Fourcade.

'It's beautiful!' Pip cried. 'You can see for miles!'

'I knew you shoulda been born a bird,' GI Joe cooed, roosting contentedly beside them, 'and what a way to travel!' He yawned and wiggled his tail feathers. 'I could get used to this.'

The afternoon drew on and when twilight blushed the clouds the landscape ahead began to change. Beyond the pastures, the stark, unmistakeable shape of buildings grew from the ground. As they multiplied, Pip shuddered, seeing the ruins of a factory that had been torn to pieces by a bombing raid some time before.

Within an hour, a sea of tall, cream houses passed beneath them, towering over open squares, long streets and wide tree-lined boulevards. Pip's eyes pored over countless chimneystacks and grey rooftops, dotted with domes and church spires, and windows stared out in all directions, mirroring the soft pink and fuchsia sky above.

'Paris!' Madame Fourcade beamed.

'Well, I'll be damned,' GI Joe cooed. 'I've never seen it in a sunset like this. She's pleased to see you, liddle lady!'

Happiness rose inside Pip at seeing a city again. She had left London to find Noah's Ark only a few weeks before, yet it felt like a lifetime ago. As much as she liked her new home in the countryside with her friends, she was an urban mouse, used to the hustle and bustle of a city; the sound of footsteps on pavements, jingling bells on doors, horns on cars and rumblings of buses. It wasn't until now that she realized how much she'd missed it, and she wished with all her heart that Mama and Papa could be with her now to see Paris for themselves.

The seagulls descended and giddiness gripped Pip's insides as she eyed the metropolis below. Some roads were blocked as men, women and children piled furniture, sandbags and debris across them, and bright awnings covered café and shop doorways along streets papered with written posters that she couldn't make out. Men and women were stopping to read them and furtively rushing across the pavements on foot or gliding away on bicycles.

There were almost no cars passing them. Instead horses or bicycles pulled small carriages, and, as Pip's gaze drifted over beautiful monuments and buildings, she swallowed, spotting huge scarlet swastika flags, billowing above them in the evening breeze.

'Look!' GI Joe pointed his wing to the right where a latticed iron tower shaped like an elongated letter 'A' loomed over the tallest buildings.

Pip gaped, recognizing it at once. 'The Eiffel Tower!'

'When Paris fell and the enemy tried to claim it as their own –' Madame Fourcade grinned – 'the French Resistance cut the wires to the elevators to ensure Hitler could never reach its summit. And when the invaders climbed it to fly their hideous flag, the humans said it was so big it blew away. But what really happened was that the birds in the animal Resistance pecked it down and it was carried away by the wind.'

Pip giggled with Madame Fourcade and GI Joe as they passed the tower, devoid of any flag.

'Do you think the humans will ever know how much animals have helped them fight the war?' Pip wondered out loud.

'They would never believe it, *chérie*!' Madame Fourcade laughed. 'Aha!' She pointed her paw to the left of the river, where a vast stone arch stood in the middle of a huge roundabout. 'That's the Arc de Triomphe! It honours those who have fought and died in wars since the French Revolution to the First World War.'

Pip looked down at a huge circle with twelve leafy boulevards stretching from it into the city beyond, and she felt a tug in her chest, reminded of Amélie hanging from her spider's web with her legs splayed out around her.

'Look!' Pip cried, spotting a mass of tanks and trucks, winding round the arch and speeding down a leafy boulevard ahead. The flight of gulls darted their heads towards it, and filled the air with excited *yeow*s.

'That's more than your average army battalion,' GI Joe cooed.

'They're heading east,' Madame Fourcade added. 'They could be in retreat! Fewer soldiers mean an easier liberation! Hurry to the white mouse in the catacombs!'

The seagulls burst forward over the Paris rooftops past the domed, ornate roof of the Grand Palais and continued following the River Seine, flowing under bridges, past men and women ambling home along the promenades for curfew. Some stopped to talk to one another and their paces were energized after each encounter. Pip felt butterflies in her stomach, feeling sure good news was spreading.

The gulls approached a large square with a tall obelisk pointing into the sky between two ornate fountains, and swerved sharply to the right past the great gilded dome of Napoleon's tomb. On and on they flew over countless chimneystacks and streets peppered with more people constructing home-made roadblocks, and as Pip spotted a big bronze lion with a proud regal face staring into the city from the middle of a large road junction, the birds began to sink lower in the sky. They continued south, a verdant green park soon appearing, and a few minutes later they plunged below the treeline and arrived in a corridor with a narrow, disused train track stretching deep beneath the streets above it: La Petite Ceinture.

Rugged walls covered with creepers towered over wildflowers, and long grass grew around the timber rail sleepers, running into a black tunnel with a speck of sunset glowing at the far end. Passing through a waterfall of ivy cascading over the opening, the seagulls swooped inside and landed in the gloom.

'Where are we?' Pip asked, hearing staccato drips of water thudding nearby as they dismounted the gulls, still grasping the umbrella between their beaks.

'No history lessons now.' Claude waddled forward. 'This place attracts unsavoury animals.' The other gulls *kek-kek*ed with unease. 'Follow me. One of many secret entrances to the catacombs is this way.'

It was then that a strange guttural cackle sounded in the tunnel ahead and Pip and her friends stiffened, their eyes roving wildly around the gloom. A dry, rasping growl sounded and the seagulls encircled Pip, Madame Fourcade and GI Joe in a barrier of outstretched wings and sharp beaks.

'Show yourself!' Claude cawed, his pales eyes squinting in the darkness. 'Now!'

'*Show yourself!*' the creature echoed. '*Now!*'

A jittery feeling of dread swept over Pip as a sinister scratching sounded ahead, and she edged closer to Madame Fourcade, trembling beside her.

'SHOW YOUR—'

'ARRRRRRGH!' the creature suddenly screeched, rocketing upwards in a cloud of dirt, and the seagulls leaped into the air in a deafening din that reverberated around the tunnel.

Pip, Madame Fourcade and GI Joe held their breaths, hearing guffaws of laughter fill the gloom. A strike of a match fizzed and, as its flame settled, it illuminated a gap in the train tracks where a timber sleeper had been levered open with a pole from below. Sitting with their legs dangling into the hole, were a mouse and a raven, holding burning matches and throwing their heads back in a fit of giggles. An African Grey parrot landed in a clatter of wings beside them and relief flooded through Pip and her friends when they realized the menacing creature was really just a group of pranksters.

'Leo?' Claude scowled. 'Is that you, you rogue?'

'I couldn't resist.' the mouse chuckled breathlessly. 'Philippe and I saw you arrive. It was too easy.'

The parrot's head bobbed with laughter. 'We just got here ourselves.'

'Don't give me that look, Claude. Think of poor Max!' Leo's Italian voice was musical, warm and mischievous. He wrapped his paw around the raven sitting beside him. 'He keeps watch all day and all night waiting for something to happen – he deserves a little thrill.'

'It's meant to be a secret entrance, Leo,' Claude scolded. 'Your little *thrill* has created enough noise to wake the dead.'

'It won't need to be secret for much longer.' Leo smiled. 'Haven't you heard? Our liberation is nearing! The Parisians have been called to arms! Posters are all over the city.'

Pip thought of the people she had seen reading papers pasted in the streets, and a flutter of excitement rose inside her.

'The battle began early and the enemy is weak,' continued Leo. 'A flimsy ceasefire has been agreed which is giving the Allied armies more time to near Paris. The Axis troops are using it to retreat, but the Parisians are trying to block the main routes with barricades!

The humans are building them all over the city, just like they did in the French Revolution, and we're going to help them win the fight when the uprising starts again! We'll kick the stinking Nazis out of Paris and France, and then the rest of Europe! The war will be over soon!'

'Don't get cocky, Leo.' Claude glared down his beak at the mouse. 'We haven't won the war yet.'

'You're just upset because we scared you –' Leo winked – 'but it didn't do you any harm. Your pride is a little bruised, that's all. We must remember how to laugh in wartime!'

Pip couldn't remember the last time she'd really laughed about anything; she wondered if she ever could after everything that had happened.

'Enough of this,' Claude interrupted. 'You're wasting our time. Let us into the catacombs.'

'*Exactement*,' Madame Fourcade added. 'We must start sabotaging the enemy at once!'

'Who's that you're hiding?' Max frowned, not recognizing the hedgehog's voice.

Opening a square of card on the floor beside him, he tore out a fresh match. He lit it from the one that had almost burned away, threw the other into the hole to expire, and walked urgently over to the gulls.

'*Mamma mia!*' Leo cursed in Italian, his own match burning his paw. He tossed the charred remains to the ground and hopped up to follow the raven with Philippe.

'Show yourself!' Max squawked, feathers ruffling nervously.

Pip held her breath as the seagulls parted. Max stared at her and the two seagulls holding the umbrella in their bills. He gazed at Madame Fourcade, GI Joe, then back at Pip and the umbrella, and his beak fell open.

'Is that . . . ?' Max's beak gaped with disbelief. 'But I thought the Umbrella Mouse was just a story.'

'My name is Pip Hanway.' Pip impatiently flicked her tail. She was sick of everyone knowing who she was but not knowing who she really was at all. 'I'm a member of Noah's Ark and we're fighting to help the Allies win the war, just like the rest of the Resistance. Then I am going to find the rest of my family, who live in the only umbrella museum in the world in Gignese, Italy.'

'That's close to my home in Lake Maggiore!' Leo's big ears popped up in surprise.

Pip ignored him, her hackles rising in irritation. 'We've travelled for days. It's been a long and difficult journey. We're tired and hungry and we must find the white mouse in the catacombs. We need you to take us to her *now*!'

A startled silence radiated around the tunnel and Pip's cheeks flushed with anger as Max, Leo and Philippe blinked, not knowing what to say.

'O-o-of course,' Max stuttered at last, turning to the gap in the railway sleepers and beckoning with his wing for the others to follow. 'Right this way.'

'Well said, kid.' GI Joe smiled with pride beside her.

Pip immediately bit her lip with embarrassment. Her temper always flared when she needed food and a good night's sleep.

'No need to look like that, *mademoiselle*,' Claude added. 'It's about time somebody taught them a lesson.'

Claude ordered the rest of the gulls back to the colony while Max guided Pip, Madame Fourcade, GI Joe, Leo and Philippe into the secret opening beneath the narrow railway sleeper. With Claude's help, they lowered the umbrella into the hole. As the seagull hopped inside after it, Max lit a fresh match, jumped after them and snatched away the pole that held the trapdoor open. Slamming shut, it clicked seamlessly into place, returning to just another of the long line of timber sleepers running through the abandoned tunnel.

*

From behind a crumbling brick left beside the disused railway track many years before, a pair of gleaming red eyes narrowed, watching Pip and her friends disappear into the gloom. With a sniff, the Goliath Rat scuttled to the secret doorway and collected the charred remains of Leo's match in its bony paws.

CHAPTER FOURTEEN

THE CROSSING

'Wait!' Max cried after Pip, Madame Fourcade and GI Joe, carrying the umbrella as they followed the seagulls down a dark, steep slope into the catacombs. Leo and Philippe the parrot turned when the raven hurled a matchbox card in their direction. It bounced off Leo's head before landing beside Pip's paws. The word *Libération* was printed beneath a picture of three flags: the British Union Jack, the American Stars and Stripes and the French Tricolour. 'You'll need one of these!'

'Ah! *Si! Grazie.*' Leo pulled out a pink-tipped match and a white spark flashed before an orange flame billowed in the gloom.

'If you hurry,' Max added, 'it should last for as long as you need it.'

'*Andiamo!*' Leo cried, leading the way down a well-trodden path deep underground.

The flare rippled above Leo's head and long shadows danced across the domed ceiling of the large chalky burrow.

'Now there's something you don't see every day,' GI Joe said as Leo scampered round a corner and skidded to a halt in front of a wall of human skulls jamming the tunnel, and Pip shivered, gazing at the empty eye sockets and toothy grins of humans long dead.

'You've seen nothing yet,' Leo said, dropping the flare on the ground upon a pile of charred matches, whittled and twisted by fire. A moment later, the flame snuffed out and plunged them into darkness.

'Now what?' Pip stared blindly into the gloom, feeling her heart begin to pound.

'Just you wait,' Philippe said behind her.

A clunk sounded, followed by a long creak, and Pip blinked in disbelief, seeing a shaft of light creep over them. Leo's silhouette came into view, pulling a tooth in the bottom left skull and opening its face as though it were a door. Behind it, a long passage sloped deeper underground, lit by a string of little electric Christmas lights fixed to the ceiling.

'Welcome to the empire of death!' Leo's eyes twinkled mischievously in the half-light and the animals' noses twitched, smelling damp air. 'It's a limestone labyrinth winding right beneath the feet of the Parisians! Six million of them are buried here and some bones are over a thousand years old.'

Pip pretended not to be scared and held her head high, hoping the tiny tremor of her whiskers did not betray her unease.

'After you, Pipsqueak!' Leo winked. Pip frowned, not liking the name at all. He couldn't be much older than she was. She walked through the skull door with Madame Fourcade, GI Joe and the umbrella without giving him a second glance.

'Will you never learn, Leo?' Claude waddled after them, ducking his head as he went. 'She's too clever for you. You'll have to try harder than that.'

'She's on to you, *mon ami*.' Philippe chuckled, padding past Leo. Sighing, Leo let go of the tooth and darted into the secret passage with the skull door swinging closed behind him.

They followed the lights into the catacombs through tunnels flecked with fossils of ancient sea creatures. It wasn't long before the path levelled and they found themselves inside a large chamber encased in beige stone, gleaming with droplets of moisture. A pool of still water lay ahead with a broad channel leading to the right. The string of little lights diverted sharply along its wall, illuminating a narrow footpath leading into the darkness beyond.

'That's where we need to go.' Leo pointed his paw to the opposite side of the pool where a tiny ledge was just visible in the shadows. 'You can't see it from here, but there's a corridor over there.'

'But shouldn't we follow the lights?' Pip asked, feeling comforted by their glow shimmering over the water.

'That's exactly what we want you to do,' Philippe said.

'If you were an intruder,' Leo added, 'you'd assume the lights would guide you to our secret hideout. Seeing your way makes a route seem safer, but that passage leads into the depths of the labyrinth from which you would never return.' Pip's eyes widened and Leo smiled, getting the reaction he wanted. 'Sometimes the right path is the least inviting.'

'How do we get across?' Madame Fourcade stared at the gloomy ledge. 'It's a long swim to the other side.'

'You don't want to swim in there!' Philippe shuddered. 'A catfish the size of a human prowls beneath the surface.'

Pip stared into the murky water and the fur on the back of her neck stood on end.

Leo went over to the parrot, who offered his wing for

the mouse to climb. 'We can't be sure where it is, so we must always fly across.'

'No need to look so worried, *mes amis*.' Claude ruffled his feathers with impatience as Pip, Madame Fourcade and GI Joe glanced at one another nervously. 'Philippe and I can carry you and your umbrella across. We've flown over it many times before.'

'Wait.' Leo followed Pip's gaze and understood what was bothering her. 'Are you afraid for the umbrella?' Pip nodded softly and Leo stared across the pool again. 'She has a point, you know. The ledge is too small for a pair of birds to land. The corridor is also too narrow to carry the umbrella side by side, and if any of us land on the water we risk being the catfish's supper.'

Claude waggled his tail feathers, knowing Leo was right.

'I know! We can float across!' Pip's eyes twinkled at Madame Fourcade and GI Joe, frowning beside her. 'In the umbrella! I'll show you – point its tip towards the water's edge.'

The hedgehog and the pigeon followed her instructions and Pip ran her paw over the umbrella's ornate silver handle. Pressing one of the fig leaves etched into the metal, the umbrella canopy instantly burst open with its handle bolting up from the ground at an angle.

'Now all we have to do –' Pip smiled – 'is push it into the water and we'll sail across. As long as a giant catfish can't eat a whole umbrella?' Pip swallowed, trying not to think of it lurking beneath the surface. Her friends glanced uneasily at one another, brows furrowed. 'Can it?'

A silence followed as the animals considered her plan.

'It's the only way to get the umbrella and all of us across safely,' Madame Fourcade sighed at last.

'But we've gotta be damn sure to get you over there before that catfish realizes what's happening, and if you wanna put to sea then you've gotta have wind in your sails.' GI Joe cooed, and all eyes darted to him. 'I'm gonna push you along with my wings.'

'But, GI,' Pip said, looking his thin frame up and down, 'are your wings strong enough?'

'I've gotta try.' GI Joe's feathers ruffled around his neck and Leo and Philippe glanced at one another nervously. 'We haven't come this far to lose you and your umbrella to an overgrown fish. So I'm gonna get you over there as fast as we can.'

'Two birds are faster than one.' Philippe stepped forward, with Leo nodding enthusiastically beside him.

'And I'll keep guard,' Claude said.

'All right, then.' Pip swallowed, trying to squash her heart thumping in her throat. 'Help me push the umbrella into the water.'

As soon as it made contact, Pip and Madame Fourcade leaped into the middle of the umbrella's open canopy and the handle righted itself over their heads. At once, their weight pushed the umbrella across the surface, rippling with tiny little waves, and Pip shivered, feeling the cool water bob beneath her paws. Unable to see over the side of the canopy curving up around them, Pip and Madame Fourcade gazed at Claude circling above, his eyes boring into the surface of the water. The hedgehog took Pip's paw in her own and gave it a reassuring squeeze.

'Here we come!' GI Joe cried, his clattering wings echoing in the chamber.

He landed unsteadily on the handle, and Pip and Madame Fourcade struggled to keep their balance as the umbrella lurched on the water in a sickening sway from side to side. Once the rocking ceased, Philippe launched into the air and wrapped his claws round the umbrella's metal pole, and Pip and Madame Fourcade stumbled as the umbrella surged across the water with the force of the pigeon and the parrot's wings.

'It's working!' Leo cried from Philippe's back. 'We'll

reach the other side in no time.'

But as Pip and Madame Fourcade beamed at one another, the seagull circling overhead suddenly screeched.

'It's coming!' Claude cried, his stony eyes widening towards the channel behind them where a long tail fin sliced the surface of the water, coming swiftly towards them. 'Hurry!' he cawed. 'It's heading straight for you!'

Pip's heart drummed behind her ribs. Without looking back, GI Joe and Philippe frantically beat their wings and dragged the umbrella over the pool. A few terrifying moments later, the birds crashed upon the narrow footpath on the other side of the chamber and slammed the metal handle and pole against the ledge. The umbrella abruptly tipped on its side, and Pip and Madame Fourcade raced from the canopy to safety.

'Get away from the umbrella!' Claude shrieked, hovering above a monstrous black shape rising out of the water.

'No!' Pip cried, rushing to the handle. 'We have to get it out!' GI Joe hurried to her with Philippe, Madame Fourcade and Leo, and as each of them snatched a piece of the umbrella Pip yelled, 'PULL!'

The animals threw themselves backwards and Claude plunged through the air as the wide, gaping mouth of the catfish lunged at them. The gull's sharp yellow beak stabbed its slimy, black skin and the fish belched, its speckled body

thrashing in pain. A moment later, it snapped its empty, long-whiskered jaws shut and slithered back below the surface of the pool.

'And stay there!' Claude spat, landing on the ledge with a waggle of his tail feathers.

'Now that was an adventure!' Leo grinned, staring breathlessly at the murky water, with Pip and the others lying in a heap and holding the dripping umbrella, doming over them as though they were sheltering from the rain.

'I don't like this place.' Pip grumbled. 'We've travelled a long way to help the humans liberate Paris and the last thing we need is to be attacked by a monster.'

Madame Fourcade nodded. 'I couldn't have put it better myself.'

'The white mouse isn't much further,' Philippe said. 'You'll see.'

CHAPTER FIFTEEN

THE PARIS RESISTANCE

Pip pressed a different button, hidden in the carved silver fig leaves on the handle, and collapsed the umbrella canopy above their heads. Letting the umbrella topple like a falling tree, she and her friends caught it in their paws and wings, and followed Leo and Philippe into the gloom.

The large limestone tunnel soon changed from rough walls to stacks of bones and skulls, which watched them pass with hollow stares and macabre smiles.

'They say this poor soul died of leprosy.' Leo stopped in front of a cracked and crumbling face.

A chill rippled down Pip's spine as Leo reached out his paw and knocked on its pitted cheekbone three times, before pausing and striking his knuckles once more. A moment later, a scuttling sounded inside the skull.

'*Ciao*, Eduardo, Céline,' Leo said, smiling, as two voles

popped out of the right eye socket.

'We have good news from the west,' Claude squawked.

'We need to see the white mouse,' Pip added, Madame Fourcade and GI Joe standing tall beside her.

'Come in!' Eduardo squeaked cheerily, spotting the little mouse carrying the umbrella. His whiskers twitched excitedly on his cheeks. 'We have been expecting you!'

The voles disappeared and the skull sank into the wall of bones with a creak of rotating wheels. Pip's mouth fell open as she stared through a mist of dust at a vast chamber bustling with life under the dim glow of little electric lights strung along the walls inside.

The animals entered the Resistance's hideout and hesitated for a moment as a one-eyed Jack Russell terrier and pair of tall, muscular rats clutching sharp, pointed spears of wood eyed them up and down with twitching noses. Satisfied Pip and her friends were not a threat, they stepped aside and watched the animals carry the umbrella into the enormous square room. The voles rumbled the skull back into place behind them and Pip's stomach growled, spying a large cluster of mushrooms growing in the corner of the room to her left. Continuing past a wall of tinned sardines, ham and vegetables stacked on top of one another, the air thrummed with the *dit*s and *dah*s of Morse code.

To the left of the chamber, a variety of small birds wearing little black headphones sat on halved wine corks under desks made from old cotton reels. In their wings, they held small rectangular triggers strung to little crystal radios. Tapping them with their faces scrunching up in concentration, they sent secret messages and scribbled replies on little bits of paper, foraged from waiters' notepads. Alongside the radio operators, a group of fifty mice and rats pedalled little bicycles fixed to the ground. Every back wheel had its tyre replaced with a belt wrapped round its metal rim and a small rotary device attached to a box. Wires snaked from each one and climbed the walls to the Christmas lights illuminating the chamber, and Pip gasped with wonder as she realized the bicycles were generating electricity.

'They're vital during power cuts.' Leo smiled, noticing her awed expression. 'We have them almost every day now. We get our electricity from Colonel Rol's bunker next door. He's a human leader of the Paris Resistance and he uses bicycles to power his hideout when the lights go out and the radios are silenced. We do the same to help him keep it running. You see those coypus over there?' Leo pointed his paw towards the opposite side of the chamber where a pair of beaver-rats, just like

Madame Fourcade had described, were sitting on their haunches with their ears pricked towards the broad end of a large speaking trumpet that was connected to a hole in the wall by its mouthpiece. 'They listen in to Colonel Rol's bunker all day and night so we're always aware of movements above ground. Then we know the best way to strike the enemy!'

Beside the coypus, a huge ornate spider's web was draped around a Red Cross flag hanging on the right-hand wall of the chamber. Beneath it, an assortment of empty food tins were cut lengthwise into cradles, creating a large medical ward that merged into a further dormitory of beds. Lined up in rows, they bulged with soft feathers, tucked in with a little sheet made from old handkerchiefs.

As they walked to the middle of the room, past a tea stall made from a broken carriage clock laid on its side, a shimmer of fireflies hovered above the biggest group of animals Pip had ever seen: mice, chickens, rats, ravens, coypus, beavers, bats, pigeons, sparrows, squirrels, rabbits, small dogs and cats all muttered to one another as they collected in front of a stage made from upright tins labelled with the word *Tomates* printed in curling red letters. Two burly rats guarded each corner, and a large map of Paris stood on an easel in the centre, where a ginger cat and a small, scruffy stray dog with very short legs and a long body talked heatedly to a white mouse whose hazel eyes blazed with life.

'Look!' a voice suddenly cried from the crowd. 'It's Pip, GI Joe and Madame Fourcade!'

At once a wave of ears pricked as all furry and feathered heads whipped round to watch the new arrivals pad across the chamber with the umbrella. The crowd promptly dispersed and the birds at the radios and the mice and rats pedalling the bicycle generators looked up for a moment and smiled, knowing the Umbrella Mouse had finally arrived, before diligently returning to their work.

A number of animals hopped from different directions through the throng, and Pip beamed, recognizing familiar faces from Noah's Ark and the Maquis. Noah's Ark's largest rabbit was the first to meet them, closely followed by a beaver with his wife and son, and the umbrella dropped on the floor as the animals embraced one another. Monique the ermine and Pie the magpie, carrying Amélie the spider on his back, were next to arrive, with the fireflies floating overhead and the two bats whirring high above them. So often in wartime, to part with one's friends meant never seeing them again, and to reunite brought a rush of hope to the animals' hearts that they could survive more dark days ahead.

'How wonderful to see you looking more like yourself, *mon ami*!' the rabbit said, affectionately patting GI Joe on the back.

'The last time we saw you, we weren't sure you were going to make it,' the beaver added, with his wife and son nodding beside him.

'Me too, buddy,' GI Joe cooed as Noah's Ark's tabby cat and squirrels approached with their tails bouncing behind them as they bounded over on all fours. 'If it wasn't for some friends we made along the way –' he smiled at the members of the Maquis, who beamed in return – 'I'd've been a goner.'

'We were starting to worry you would miss the battle.' The cat pressed her forehead to Madame Fourcade's and the hedgehog smiled broadly. 'The humans are rising up on the streets of Paris.'

'And we shall help them triumph.' The hedgehog's eyes shone with tears of relief, seeing her troop safe and well. 'Is Noah's Ark all accounted for?' she asked the cat, her voice hushed with concern.

'The mice are yet to arrive,' the cat replied sombrely. 'The rats lost them in the forest.'

'We must not think the worst.' Madame Fourcade patted a reassuring paw on the cat's fur, but Pip noticed her eyes glaze with worry. 'It was an arduous journey for us all. They could still emerge.'

'We were wondering when you'd get here!' said a

squirrel, grinning at Pip as she and two others squeezed her inside a warm hug.

The large crowd of animals inside the chamber surrounded them now, murmuring excitedly to one another with twitching noses and ears. Behind them, the white mouse zigzagged her way through the throng, closely followed by the scruffy stray dog and the ginger cat.

The white mouse chuckled, clutching Pip's paw in both of her own and shaking it fondly. 'The mouse that beat the invaders on their own turf! Fair dinkum! We meet at last!' Her voice was kind yet firm, and Pip sensed the fearlessness of the bigger mouse. She liked her at once. 'I'm Nancy and I'm in charge of this rabble of Resistance groups, along with this dog and cat.' The scruffy stray dog and the ginger cat nodded in greeting and sat on their haunches. 'I'm here to help as a member of Churchill's Secret Animal Army, just like you,' Nancy continued. 'Those old cobbers of ours in London are going to be pleased to know you've found us. They've been asking about you morning, noon and night.'

'Cobbers?' Pip's brow furrowed.

'Our mates in London: Bernard Booth and Dickin.' Nancy chuckled and Pip grinned, thinking of her dear friend. The white mouse gave her a little wink and turned to the hedgehog. 'And, Madame Fourcade, it's a pleasure to put a face to your Morse code.'

'I hope my radio operator arrived ahead of us?' The hedgehog darted her eyes over the group of birds to the left of the room.

'Robert's here.' Nancy pointed her paw to the bullfinch, feverishly tapping Morse code beside a beautiful kingfisher with a bright orange body and turquoise wings. 'He's firing messages alongside Noor, one of the finest operators in Churchill's Secret Animal Army. She's the first female wireless operator sent into France and she does a bloody good job of it too.'

'Nancy,' Claude interrupted, and the white mouse turned her gaze to the gull. 'My scouts have seen the human Allied army win the battle around Falaise in the west. They're advancing east so there's a real chance they'll come to Paris's aid.'

'And we met sky-dogs on our journey too,' Pip added, excitement popping the whiskers on her cheeks. 'They were sent to stop any counter-attacks against the Allied army and to help any Resistance group they can.'

'This confirms it,' said the scruffy dog, smiling beside Nancy. 'With the Allied landings in the south, victory to the west and advances into the north of France, we are successfully pushing the enemy back into Germany! Our liberation is at hand!'

All the animals in the chamber stirred with excitement.

'Claude,' Nancy ordered. 'Go back to your colony, keep track of the Allied progress to the outside of Paris and report back to us tomorrow.'

The gull nodded and promptly waddled out of the hideout. At the same moment, the kingfisher let out a gasp and ripped her headphones from her ears. Darting her head this way and that in search of the white mouse, Noor spread her brightly coloured wings and fluttered across the chamber while the other birds behind her continued tapping Morse code.

'I have a message from Bernard Booth!' Noor cried, speaking rapidly as she landed beside them. Pip gazed up at her, transfixed by the flash of orange around her eyes and the vivid feathers speckled in different hues of blue around her head. 'He is delighted you have found us, Pip and Madame Fourcade, but, Nancy,' she said, grinning, 'Bernard believes the ceasefire and the evacuation of Axis personnel indicates the enemy is weak, but even if only a scant amount of troops remain in Paris, their weapons will still outnumber the Resistance's. Without military aid from the Allied armies, the uprising could fail and Hitler could retaliate. He says we must sabotage everything we can – *now*, under the cover of darkness – and do our best to undermine the enemy before the uprising starts again. The weaker they are, the more chance the insurgence will hold long enough for the Allied armies to arrive.'

'The Resistance radio station is broadcasting!' Robert the bullfinch cried out, and at once the raven hurried over to him and bent his ears to his headphones. 'It's a weak signal, but the humans are telling the Parisians to rise up again!'

The ginger cat's pupils dilated with excitement. 'The ceasefire won't hold for much longer.'

'Then what are we waiting for?' The white mouse's eyes blazed as she called out to the animals in the chamber.

'My friends, the time has come!' the dog cried. The animals quietened with their ears pricked. 'After years of oppression, we are going to kick the Nazis back to Berlin! Get into your groups and head into the city. Those who itch: spread your fleas! Those who know engines: chew through the fuel and engine lines of every enemy vehicle and tank you can lay your paws on, and take candle wax with you to seal up the holes! Cats: hunt every Goliath Rat you can find, and everyone with teeth – rip through *anything* as long as it undermines the power of the invaders! The rat and raven guards will be securing this hideout while you are away, and we will welcome you back with victory ringing in our ears! Now go! And fight bravely! Our freedom is at hand!'

Pip's heart stirred as all the animals in the chamber roared with enthusiasm and huddled together into their different factions to organize sabotage missions.

'Noah's Ark!' Madame Fourcade cried as the animals gathered around the hedgehog and the umbrella with their eyes glowing with determination. 'We must set out at once. Leo, Philippe,' she said, spotting them glance at the group and shuffle awkwardly, 'are you joining us?'

'We would be delighted, Madame!' Leo beamed and Pip was surprised to feel her cheeks flame.

'Their wit and wings will be a great help,' Nancy said, smiling, padding over to the group, and Leo and Philippe stood taller with their eyes twinkling with pride. 'I've known their tricks since they joined the Resistance in Marseille.'

'*Du Stinkstiefel!*' Philippe the parrot barked.

Pip, Madame Fourcade and GI Joe gaped in astonishment.

'You can speak *human*?' Pip's ears pricked, listening to Philippe utter German in a throaty human voice. 'What did you just say?'

'I said *You smelly boot*,' Philippe chuckled.

'It's his favourite German phrase,' Leo chortled, 'and he's learned many more since the enemy arrived four years ago.'

'He's our resident comedian,' Nancy added. 'He's had the Resistance in stitches over the years.'

'Do you ever use your speech to distract the humans?' Pip said, her mind tingling with ideas.

'When the time is right.' Philippe met her gaze and their eyes twinkled with mischief. 'I entertained guests at a hotel bar,' the parrot added. 'The more I made them laugh, the kinder my owner was to me.'

'He was a brute.' Leo scowled. 'Philippe was so scared of him he used to pluck out his feathers when he came near. So one night my little sister and I chewed through the hinges to his cage door and set him free. We've been friends ever since.'

'*Génial!* And where is your little sister now?' Madame Fourcade asked.

'When Mussolini joined Hitler in 1940, my family moved to Marseille with the old artist we lived with in Lake Maggiore,' Leo replied. 'We stowed away inside his suitcase and we had many adventures together.' He sighed. 'Until I lost them all in a bombing raid – an Italian one! Can you believe it? I'll only go back to Italy when the Allies have won the war.'

A sad silence unfurled around the animals as Leo hung his head. Pip ached for him. He'd lost his family in the same way she had and she immediately felt closer to him, sharing a mutual sorrow that words could never describe. They were both orphans trying to find their way home, and knowing him somehow made her feel closer to her mother's family in Gignese.

'Hard times make us fiercer fighters,' Nancy said at last, giving Pip a wink. 'Count me in, Noah's Ark. I know just the sabotage for us.'

Pip and her friends' ears pricked, and the white mouse grinned mischievously.

'We're going into the belly of the beast: the enemy's military headquarters.'

CHAPTER SIXTEEN

HÔTEL LE MEURICE

After a feast of catacomb mushrooms and tinned sardines, with the rest of the animal Resistance energetically discussing their sabotage missions, Pip left the umbrella in the care of Robert the bullfinch and the other radio operators, and clambered on to Philippe's back with Madame Fourcade. They followed Nancy, Leo and GI Joe, leading the way through the labyrinth of limestone corridors, lit by another long string of little electric bulbs.

It wasn't long before they landed again beside a towering pile of rubble, lying in disarray where a wall had collapsed many years before. A dark triangular opening was hidden behind it, and as the white mouse guided the animals through it Pip glanced over her shoulder at the lights, distracting any would-be followers away from the secret passage and further into the maze beyond.

The darkness inside the opening swallowed them whole. For what seemed like hours, the animals trod blindly up a steep burrow, tripping now and again on the uneven ground. Just as Pip felt their climb would never end, the track softened beneath her paws, and the pungent smell of earth seeped into her nose.

'Help me with this door,' Nancy said as the path came to an abrupt end, and Pip's ears twitched, feeling little spindly roots tickle them from above.

They were all dusted with falling soil as they pressed against the ceiling and lifted a loosened plant. As it collapsed gently on its side, their lungs were filled with fresh air, and Pip and the others blinked at a sprinkling of stars glittering around murky clouds above.

'Come on,' Nancy whispered, leading the animals out of the hole into a flower bed filled with white and pink peonies in bloom. Pip clambered after her and looked up at a tall marble statue of an angel gazing into the distance beside verdant trees stirring in a humid, summer breeze.

'GI Joe,' Nancy whispered as the animals replaced the uprooted peony plant in the ground and hid the opening to the catacombs from view. 'Follow us to the Hôtel Le Meurice. On a night like tonight, the windows will be open to cool the men sleeping in their beds. We'll creep inside and wreak as much havoc as we can.'

'Let's go.' Pip smiled, excitement overtaking the tiredness that had clung to her over the last few days. This sabotage sounded easy, and after all the years she'd spent exploring the James Smith & Sons umbrella shop in London she was looking forward to being inside a building again.

The birds leaped into the air with a burst of their wings and soared over treetops and formal gardens decorated with statues towering over colourful flowers. Ahead, enemy soldiers armed with rifles guarded the Luxembourg Palace, silhouetted in the moonlight. Its white clockface struck two as the animals flew silently over the palace's bell tower and Pip's heart stirred, spying two squirrels spiralling up its flagpole. A moment later, a scarlet swastika flag rippled and fell through the summer breeze, and Pip and her friends beamed with pride.

The birds continued north and Pip's eyes widened at the boulevards below. Men and women were defying sleep and working through the night, prising up paving stones, pickaxing cobbled streets and piling the debris across the roads. Further down the street, a tree fell and crashed against the tarmac. Pip and her friends chuckled with glee, seeing the dark shapes of the beavers scurrying away to the nearby River Seine, shimmering by the light of the moon under bridges connecting the left and right banks of the city.

Soaring across the water, Philippe and GI Joe passed over an elaborate arch crowned with four bronze horses pulling a chariot, and cut across the manicured Tuileries Gardens. Pip smiled, spotting a flash of a magpie's black-and-white feathers, flying over a row of Tiger tanks parked on the grass to their left, and they arrived at a six-storey building with three red flags gently billowing above its grand front entrance. The words *Hôtel Le Meurice* were mounted in gold to balcony railings wrapped around its first floor, where the French doors were cracked ajar, just as Nancy had predicted.

'Pip, Leo, come with me,' Nancy whispered, slipping off GI Joe's back on to the balcony with her eyes roving over the building. The mice nodded and dismounted from the birds. 'We're the only ones small enough to squeeze under the doors inside.'

'We'll do the rooms upstairs while you three tackle down here,' GI Joe cooed, craning his neck upwards with the others.

'Damage papers, telephone cords, radios – whatever you can see that could hinder the enemy's efforts,' Madame

Fourcade ordered from Philippe's back, 'and keep an eye out for any information we can use against the enemy, like photographs, maps or drawings.'

Pip smiled at her friends. 'Good luck!'

'We'll meet you back here when we're done –' Madame Fourcade's eyes blazed – 'and be careful!'

With that, GI Joe and Philippe took to the air with Madame Fourcade, and disappeared into an open window on the second floor.

Pip, Nancy and Leo tiptoed to a crack in an open French door. Pushing their way past a net curtain, they shimmied under heavy, velvet drapes and entered a large bedroom with glass chandeliers glinting from the ceiling in the gloom. Pip gaped as her eyes travelled over ornate sconces dotted about the walls above an antique Louis XIV sofa and chairs. To their left, a low rumble of snores sounded from a bed and Pip swallowed, spying the bulbous shape of a reclining man.

'Look,' Pip whispered, pointing to a telephone on a bedside table.

Nerves coiled in her stomach as they darted across a silk rug. Keeping one eye on the man lying in the bed, they approached a black cord running from the skirting board to the telephone stand towering above their heads.

They wrapped their teeth around it, but suddenly the man uttered a loud snort, and Pip, Nancy and Leo raced under the bed. The man snuffled as he turned on his side and the mice breathed easier, edging forward again and gnawing clean through the line.

'Come on . . .' Pip's eyes were wide with adventure as she let go of the wire. 'Let's go next door!'

With Nancy and Leo at her heels, she bounded across the room and slipped under a door leading to a grand corridor with paintings hanging inside elaborate, gilded frames. Squeezing under the first door on the left, they arrived in a large room with a map of Paris leaning against the wall above a broad desk covered with documents.

The mice bolted to it and climbed a wire dangling from a gold lamp. Scaling it to the top, Pip and Nancy pored over sheets scrawled with writing while Leo nibbled through another telephone line on the other side of the table.

'Have you found anything?' Pip asked, searching the papers for any intelligence, but she couldn't make sense of the German words. Her whiskers drooped, thinking of Hans. As a German rat fighting with the Resistance, he would have loved to be with them now.

'Nothing yet.' Nancy sighed, shredding a sheet with her teeth and claws in frustration.

'What's this?' Pip's eyes fell on a detailed black-and-white drawing of a building the mice recognized at once. The word *DYNAMIT* was scribbled against each corner of its first-floor gallery.

'I don't believe it!' Leo gasped.

'They're going to blow up the Eiffel Tower!' Nancy shuddered. 'This must be the retaliation Bernard Booth suspected.'

'Not if we stop them,' Pip said, hurrying back to the lamp perched on the end of the desk. 'Quick, we have to find the others.'

Pip clambered down the cable with Nancy and Leo chasing after her, but suddenly the Hôtel Le Meurice quaked as a gargantuan gust of air blasted through Paris, and the mice tumbled to the ground.

CHAPTER SEVENTEEN

THE EIFFEL TOWER

The explosion had rocked the Hôtel Le Meurice on its foundations and Pip's mind was paralysed by memories of the bomb blast that had killed her parents and destroyed her home in London. The bloodstained bricks and broken glass flashed before her eyes and she trembled with terror, the memory of the smouldering bus on the street with flames flickering around the people inside fresh in her mind.

'Pip? Can you hear me?' a faraway voice asked. 'Are you all right, *topolina*?'

'*Topolina*?' Pip groaned, opening her eyes and finding Leo's kind face looking down at her with his brow furrowed with concern. She frowned, not understanding the last word.

'It means *little mouse*.' Leo smiled. 'Are you OK? You hit your head and fainted.'

'That crash,' she said, blinking. 'Was it a bomb?'

'We'll soon find out,' Nancy replied, urgently heaving Pip, quivering with fear, up on to unsteady paws. 'Now get your skates on. This place will be crawling with humans any minute!'

At that moment, another crash thundered outside the building and the mice threw themselves to the floor.

'Get up!' Nancy whispered, dragging Pip and Leo by the paws. 'This is no time for dawdling! Come on!'

The mice scrambled to the door and squeezed under it again, but as soon as they popped out on the other side they froze, flattening themselves against the wall. Two Goliath Rats were bounding up a grand staircase to their left. Pip held her breath until they disappeared, hearing the unmistakeable sound of humans storming through the building.

'Run!' Nancy shoved the younger mice forward.

The three dashed down the corridor and slipped back under the bedroom door with men's footsteps and voices pounding in their ears.

'Look out!' Nancy whispered, forcing Pip and Leo to a halt by the wrists and motioning her head to the man now sitting upright on the bed with his back turned to them, grappling with the telephone by the light of a silver candelabra. 'Tread *slowly*!' she added. 'Human eyes catch sight of our speed.'

'*Hallo?*' the man growled into the receiver, aggressively tapping his pudgy fingers on the cradle. The mice edged forward towards the open balcony doors. '*Hallo? HALLO?*'

The man slammed the handset back on the receiver with a jingle of its bell, and the mice darted under a chair as he cursed. With heavy footsteps shuddering the floorboards, he stormed across the room to open his bedroom door and slammed it closed behind him.

'*Was war DAS?*' he roared in German, and the mice rushed to the heavy velvet curtains with their hearts drumming in their throats.

'*Eine Explosion im Grand Palais, Herr General von Choltitz!*' Pip heard another man reply shakily as the mice arrived outside, their mouths falling open at a towering flame scorching the night.

'There you are!' Madame Fourcade's prickles bristled beside GI Joe and Philippe on the balcony.

'Is that the Grand Palais?' Pip gazed out at the blaze. 'They've just said there was an explosion there.'

'Looks like the ceasefire's gone up in smoke, liddle lady.' GI Joe sighed.

'It's terrible.' Madame Fourcade's face crumpled, gazing

at the nightmarish red glow. 'It is one of Paris's treasures.'

Nancy frowned. 'Was it an air raid?'

'We saw no planes.' Philippe shook his head sadly. 'It must have been tank shells or explosives.'

Madame Fourcade's brow furrowed, recognizing the worry creasing Pip's face. 'What's wrong?'

'We found diagrams.' Pip swallowed. 'We think the enemy is planning to blow up the Eiffel Tower.'

'*What!*' cried Madame Fourcade, GI Joe and Philippe.

'But there's no military value in destroying it!' GI Joe's feathers ruffled around his neck in outrage. 'It's madness.'

'It has symbolic significance.' Madame Fourcade shook her head in despair. 'It represents the whole of France. Destroying it will crush the French spirit.'

'Not if we stop it from happening!' Pip interrupted, paws clenched in determination. But before she could say more the door inside the bedroom banged shut and pounding footsteps charged towards them. Flinching in alarm, Pip and Madame Fourcade scrambled on to Philippe's back while Nancy and Leo leaped to GI Joe.

A clap of thunder rumbled overhead as the man ripped open the curtains and stormed on to the balcony. Staring across the Tuileries Gardens at orange flames raging inside the Grand Palais, he cursed in German, having no idea he had just missed a parrot and a pigeon who now soared over the treetops towards the River Seine.

The streets of Paris hummed with life as the birds raced west along the left bank, past men and women standing on their balconies in their nightclothes, and pointing at the inferno on the other side of the river.

Rain pitter-pattered on the animals' fur and feathers as the birds followed a broad, tree-lined boulevard running alongside the water. As they neared the Eiffel Tower, stretching high above the rooftops, Pip gazed down at the streets from Philippe's back and caught sight of two young men sprinting along the pavement. They wore white shirts rolled up around their arms. In their right hands they carried rifles, and tricolour armbands were wrapped above their left elbows. One reminded her of Peter, the son of the owner of her umbrella shop in London. His dark hair flopped in the same way around his head as his lean body charged past buildings with French flags hanging proudly from windows below. She wished with all her might that, wherever Peter was fighting the war now, he was alive and safe.

The young men raced on as a truck stuffed with enemy soldiers slowed at a junction ahead. It lurched in their direction with a screech of its tyres, and Pip peered over her shoulder to see the young men dart left through a large stone arch beneath a towering church spire. A moment later, the vehicle roared down the street, and a wave of shutters closed over the windows above as the Parisians watching the fire from their balconies hurried away from the Axis soldiers below.

The row of buildings overlooking the river abruptly came to an end and GI Joe and Philippe swooped sharply upwards to land on the last grey rooftop facing the Eiffel Tower. The animals crouched behind a chimneystack and Pip craned her neck to see the peak of the tower. It was the most gigantic thing she'd ever seen and she couldn't fathom how its hefty metal frame could stand without toppling over. Lowering her eyes, she could just make out the inside of the enormous first-floor gallery. At each corner that she could see, a silhouette of a soldier stood behind a long-barrelled machine gun.

'The diagram we found had explosives rigged to the ledge beneath those men,' she whispered as sheet lightning flashed in the distance, illuminating the clouds in electric blue. 'But I can't see where they are from here and we've got to find a way to get rid of those soldiers. We need a closer look.'

'I'll take you – a pigeon blends in better than a parrot.' GI Joe glanced at Philippe, cocking his head. 'Sorry, buddy.'

'I have other talents.' Philippe shrugged nonchalantly and instantly Pip's memory sparked with the sound of the parrot's throaty human voice.

'That's right!' she grinned. 'Philippe, do you think you can distract those soldiers while we sabotage the explosives?'

'*Oui*,' Philippe croaked, and the others looked at one another excitedly.

'Then hop on.' The pigeon cooed. 'Let's see what we can find.'

'But for whiskers' sake, *chérie*,' Madame Fourcade added as Pip settled herself behind GI Joe's neck, 'don't let those soldiers see you!'

'We'll be back before you know it.' GI Joe winked and jumped into the air.

Gunfire clattered in the city as the pigeon flew over treetops towards the Eiffel Tower. Nearing its hulking iron lattice, Pip gaped at its intricate filigree arches rising and falling between four enormous legs made from criss-crossing metal beams. Above them, a trellis of girders supported the tower's gigantic first floor. Swerving sharply to the right, GI Joe followed the lower ledge of its balcony, now thudding metallically with falling raindrops.

'I see one!' Pip cried as they approached the first corner where a massive pile of cylinders had *DYNAMIT* printed on the side with an eagle carrying a swastika. Every stick was about the size of the candles Pip had seen used at dining tables. They were taped together in four blocks and each central cylinder had a black wire protruding from it.

'Shhh,' GI Joe cooed quietly. 'Look!'

Pip bit her lip. Over their heads, an enemy soldier peered through binoculars at the flames raging inside the

Grand Palais across the River Seine. Beside him, a long barrel of a gun pointed to the bridge stretching across the water below.

The pigeon flew them anti-clockwise round the tower. Sure enough, Pip and GI Joe spied explosives placed evenly around the first floor, and each one had an enemy soldier and a machine gun aimed into the city below.

'Hurry back to the others,' Pip said as GI Joe completed his loop. 'I've got an idea!'

She stared at the Eiffel Tower over her shoulder, her fur quivering with nerves.

She hoped this was going to work.

CHAPTER EIGHTEEN

SOLDIERS

Pip and Leo's whiskers pulled on their cheeks as GI Joe charged forward beside Philippe, who was carrying Madame Fourcade and Nancy on his back. Soaring through the rain falling heavily in the gloom, they headed for the western corner of the Eiffel Tower's first-floor gallery, where a ledge jutted out from beneath the balcony.

The birds landed on its metal surface with a scratch of their claws, and Pip heaved a sigh of relief as the raindrops masked the sound. The mice and the hedgehog dismounted, with the wind blustering around their fur, and stared out at the fire flickering around the Grand Palais in the distance. A flash of sheet lightning turned the clouds violet above, and Pip lifted her head to the left where a soldier stood with his back turned and his arm resting on his machine gun.

'There it is,' Pip whispered, pointing her paw towards the man's feet, where a big pile of dynamite stood starkly against the painted iron. 'Another is strapped to the other side of this corner, and it's the same around the whole first floor. Let's disarm each one.'

'*Bonne chance, mes amis*,' Philippe said. 'I'll distract the soldiers one by one. Wait for my signal each time, then rip those wires to shreds.'

Thunder rumbled overhead as the parrot dived from the ledge and disappeared into the darkness. Minutes passed, and the animals stared nervously out over the rooftops in silence, watching bursts of explosions from distant battles that now raged in the city below.

'*Heil Hitler!*' Philippe shouted somewhere in the gloom, and Pip saw the soldier instantly turn towards the sound and salute. '*Komm her! Jetzt!*' Philippe's voice sounded again.

At once, the man obediently marched away from his post, retracing the path the animals had just made.

'It's working!' Leo whispered excitedly.

'Lead the way, young Pip,' Nancy said beside him.

Thunder crashed as Pip bounded forward, but a moment later she yelped in terror, feeling her paws skid on the wet iron.

'Don't you dare!' Madame Fourcade leaped forward, snatching her by the wrist, with Pip's hind legs dangling over brink. 'I am not losing you to a stumble after everything we have been through!'

'*Everyone* tread carefully!' Nancy ordered, helping Madame Fourcade drag Pip to safety with Leo. Pip could barely stand for the fright quaking her limbs. 'None of us are dying tonight! Have I made myself clear?' Nancy bossed, nudging the animals forward. 'Now get going! Philippe's ruse could come unstuck any minute!'

The animals hurried across the ledge as quickly as they could, listening to the parrot bark German orders into the night. A few seconds brought them to the first corner of the first-floor gallery, and GI Joe kept watch as Pip and the others climbed over the heap of explosives.

'Wait, *chérie*,' Madame Fourcade whispered urgently as Pip and Leo snatched up a black cord protruding from the centre of one of the four blocks of dynamite. She looked up at Nancy with wide eyes. 'How do we know it won't blow up when we bite the wires?'

Pip and Leo let go of the fuses at once and a fearful silence radiated around the animals. The rapid, thudding raindrops hitting the Eiffel Tower echoed Pip's heartbeat thumping in her ears.

'Dynamite is simple.' Nancy's eyes shone in the gloom. 'Cut the wires and it cannot detonate!'

Without a moment's hesitation, everyone nibbled and chewed the wires until all the fuses parted and frayed.

'*Super!*' the hedgehog cried as Pip released the last wire from her jaws.

'We've got to do this three more times before the Eiffel Tower is safe.' Pip glanced towards the next corner to their left. 'We need to carry on, but it's too dark and too far away to see if Philippe has distracted the second soldier yet – he could spot us if we get there too soon.'

'You guys keep going,' GI Joe said, flexing his wings. 'I'm gonna find out.'

'Come on!' Nancy pushed them forward as the pigeon burst into the air. 'The longer we wait, the longer those dingbats have to work out what's going on.'

The headiness of the height and the peril of the sabotage pulsed through their bodies as Pip, Leo and Madame Fourcade chased after Nancy, moving as quickly as they could across the ledge through the rain. As they neared the second heap of dynamite, their ears pricked, hearing Philippe shriek, '*Heil Hitler! Komm her!*' ahead, and at once Pip and her friends felt lighter on their paws seeing another soldier step away from the corner to follow the parrot's voice.

'Go, go, go!' GI Joe swooped alongside them with a huge smile upon his face. 'Neither of these men have wised up to what's happening!'

'Let's hope it lasts!' Nancy said as the animals arrived at the second pile of explosives and gnawed through the fuses again. Leo and Pip shredded the last wire, but suddenly the animals froze, hearing human footsteps thud past them. The first soldier was searching for the second.

'*Hallo du!*' he shouted after him.

'*Ja?*' the other replied in the darkness beyond.

'*Was ist los?*'

Pip and her friends stared at each other in dismay.

'They're on to us,' Philippe whispered, flying low and landing beside the others. His brow furrowed as his eyes darted anxiously to his friends. 'What do we do now?'

'We're halfway there,' Pip said, nerves jangling in her stomach, 'and we'll be faster if we go in two teams.'

'You're right.' Madame Fourcade nodded gravely with the others. 'But if we don't act fast they could suspect the explosives are being sabotaged, and then we've failed.' Everybody's ears flattened at her words. 'Philippe, reveal yourself to these two men so they know they have nothing to worry about. Be playful and charming. Hopefully they'll think you're just a lost pet parrot and nothing else. Then fly as fast as you can to the third soldier and distract him from his explosives in whatever way you can, before continuing to the final pile of dynamite.'

'*Bonne idée*.' Philippe spread his wings and jumped into the air crying, '*Hallo! Du bist wundervoll!*' The two soldiers instantly smiled and pointed at the parrot as he zoomed onwards to the third soldier, before they turned away and calmly walked back to their posts.

'Pip and Leo,' GI Joe added urgently as Philippe jumped into the air and disappeared into the darkness. 'I'll take you to the fourth corner while you and Nancy tackle the third, Madame.'

'Let's show these young whippersnappers how it's done.' Nancy nudged Madame Fourcade as Pip leaped on to GI Joe's back and reached out her paw for Leo to climb up. He squeezed it in thanks as he settled behind her.

'We'll meet you at the end of the road, *chérie*,' Madame Fourcade said, and Pip's chest tightened as she watched them hurry away.

'Go, GI!' Pip cried.

With a furious flap of his wings, the pigeon soared over Nancy and Madame Fourcade, bounding through the gloom towards the third soldier, who had stumbled backwards with surprise, having a parrot perched on his shoulder singing the German national anthem. Flying low, GI Joe rocketed towards the final corner and a lump rose in Pip's throat, catching a last glimpse of Madame Fourcade and Nancy racing along the ledge to jump on to the third heap of dynamite. Pip closed her eyes and made a wish that no harm would come to them.

As GI Joe completed the loop round the Eiffel Tower and headed towards the flames glowing inside the Grand Palais again, Pip's stomach plunged.

'*Geh weg!*' the last soldier cried, hurling his arm at Philippe, hopping along the ledge beside him. The parrot leaped away, squawking, '*Du Stinkstiefel!*' and circled the darkness above the man, who stubbornly ignored his insults and remained hunched over his machine gun, aimed at the bridge crossing the River Seine below.

Pip glanced over her shoulder for Madame Fourcade and Nancy, and her heart sank, finding no sign of them. Wracking her mind for a way to complete the sabotage before it was too late, suddenly her brain pinged, remembering something that had happened once with her friends Dot and Joe in London.

'All humans, no matter how big and brave, are frightened of creatures suddenly crawling over their skin,' Pip said, trying to sound as confident as possible, but, in truth, her idea made her gut churn with fear. 'I'm going to jump inside that soldier's collar and distract him while GI Joe flies you to the last explosives.'

'*What?*' GI Joe balked, wings slowing with shock.

'That's crazy, *topolina*.' Leo shook his head firmly. 'We'll wait for Nancy and Madame Fourcade, and we'll disarm the dynamite together.'

'But if this soldier sees or hears us, everything we've done will be wasted!' Pip looked over her shoulder again for the hedgehog and the white mouse, her insides thudding with worry. 'Something must have happened. It's up to us to finish this now.'

'Then let me do the soldier and you do the wires!' Leo pleaded, his voice cracking with worry.

'I've done it before and I can do it again,' she cried, speaking rapidly as GI Joe approached the final soldier. 'It happened once when my friends and I sneaked into the theatre behind the umbrella shop in London. We were trying to get a better view of the stage when I slipped and fell from one of the balconies, right into the back of a man's collar below.'

She didn't mention how terrified she'd been scuttling across his shoulders and down his sleeve to escape through the cuff of his jacket. She'd then raced under the seats, blood screaming in her ears, and her friends had tittered for days afterwards.

'It was funny. He jumped up and screamed, and the whole auditorium laughed. His wife didn't believe I was there.'

'Are you sure about this?' GI Joe asked, slowing as he considered her plan.

'Yes!' She swallowed, throat as dry as ash with every second they neared the soldier.

'No, *topolina*, I can't let you do this!' Leo said urgently. 'Like you said when we first met, you have a family to find in Italy. I have nobody. I should go!'

'That isn't true, Leo.' Pip looked over her shoulder into his kind face, and her heart stirred. 'You have us now, and Noah's Ark takes care of each other. Hurry, GI!'

'All right, liddle lady –' the pigeon fiercely beat his wings – 'but you be careful! I'll pick you up as soon as you get outta there.' She bit her lip, the soldier's fitted sage green jacket zooming ever closer. 'On the count of three.' Pip nodded, clenching her paws into fists to stop them from trembling. 'One, tw—'

But before GI Joe got to three Leo hurled himself from the pigeon's back and landed on the soldier's jacket collar with a small thump.

At once the soldier stood bolt upright and stumbled backwards with a wriggle of unease, feeling something warm and furry scuttle down the back of his neck. As Leo's cold little paws scrambled over his body, the man shrieked in alarm and hopped up and down, his hands slapping the little lump that was rippling through his uniform.

'Leo! No!' Pip cried, unable to take her eyes off the man, clawing at his jacket buttons and panting in alarm.

GI Joe dived sharply to the ledge jutting below the machine gun pointing from the balcony, and Pip rushed from his back to stare through the gaps in the balustrades, her heart hammering behind her ribs.

'That was a shock for me too!' GI Joe grabbed her by the shoulders and stared into her eyes. 'But you and I have got a job to do now. You've gotta disarm this thing and I've gotta go get that loony friend of ours outta trouble. Now go! There's no time for delay!'

He burst into the air and Pip felt a sharp stab of guilt at not being able to go to Leo's aid. But she knew GI Joe was right, and she raced to the last blocks of explosives, feverishly gnawing through every fuse until they were disarmed.

With her mind whirring for a way to help her friends, Pip held her breath, watching the soldier duck away from

GI Joe, flapping and pecking about his head. Swinging his arms, the man struck the pigeon with his fist and GI Joe faltered in the air for a moment before he circled to attack again.

The soldier writhed in disgust and ripped off his jacket with Leo still inside. Slamming it on the floor, he jumped, stamping his big, black boots all over its surface in a sinister dance that made Pip's blood freeze.

'*Mäuse!*' the soldier yelled, catching sight of Leo darting out of the sleeve.

'Hang on, Leo!' Pip cried, seeing the terror etched on his face as he dodged and weaved between the soldier's feet crashing down all around him. 'I'm coming!' But before Pip could race through the gaps between the railings she clasped her paws over her mouth in horror. The toe of the soldier's boot caught Leo in the flank and launched him over the balcony into the night beyond.

Just then, Philippe hurtled through the darkness above her head with Madame Fourcade and Nancy clinging to his back. Snatching Leo in his beak, he frantically beat his wings and swooped to the right towards the orange flames still flickering inside the Grand Palais.

GI Joe urgently landed beside her. 'Let's get the hell outta here!' Pip scrambled on to his back and he charged after Philippe, racing east over the Paris rooftops.

'Is he alive?' Pip felt sick with guilt, seeing Leo dangling limply in the parrot's mouth. It was her idea to climb into the soldier's uniform and it should have been her, not him, who had performed the task. She'd never forgive herself for not realizing he would take her place.

'We think so,' Madame Fourcade replied, and Philippe's eyes were clouded with worry, 'but he needs a doctor if he's going to survive.'

'Then we have to get him back to the catacombs,' Nancy said, 'and we need to get there fast.'

'Where's the closest entrance?' GI Joe asked.

'The flower bed where we arrived in the city before,' Nancy replied. 'All the others are further south.'

At once, Philippe and GI Joe swerved away from the River Seine and swiftly flew over chimneystacks, church spires and the gilded dome of Napoleon's tomb towards the Luxembourg Gardens. In the gloom below, Pip saw that fewer flags were flying over monuments where swastikas had billowed before and the leafy boulevards were sparser where trunks had been felled. Barricades made from bricks, old furniture, metal grating, concrete paving and fallen trees stretched across roads all over the city with people huddled behind them, holding rifles and wearing the tricolour wrapped round their upper arms. But as the birds neared the Luxembourg Palace a cold shiver of dread rippled down Pip's spine.

Thundering blasts tore through the streets nearby, kicking pockets of dust into the air and scattering men in fear. Pip spotted a Tiger tank a moment afterwards, rolling through the remains of a barricade with mist trickling from its gun barrel. As her mind raced for a way in which they could sabotage it, a flutter of black-and-white feathers dashed through the darkness and landed on its rear fuel compartment. A second later, a magpie took to the air with an ermine clinging to its back, and a rush of pride rose inside Pip and Madame Fourcade, knowing it was Pie and Monique from the Maquis.

Philippe and GI Joe neared the south side of the Luxembourg Gardens and Pip's eyes widened, spying small bursts of light blazing behind hedges and statues where men in civilian clothes engaged in a fierce gunfight with enemy soldiers.

'The stinking Nazis are shooting at the Resistance beside our flower bed!' Nancy cursed. 'There's no way we can access the catacombs from there now.'

'Where's the next closest entrance?' Pip asked urgently, glancing at Leo hanging lifelessly from Philippe's beak and feeling more worried than ever.

'La Petite Ceinture,' Nancy replied. 'The abandoned railway tunnel.'

'The one guarded by Max the raven?' Madame Fourcade asked.

Nancy nodded with Philippe. 'Yes, there's a secret door under one of the sleepers.'

'We know it,' GI Joe said, robustly flapping his wings with the parrot. 'That's how we came in first. Leo, you hang on, buddy! We'll be there soon!'

The birds charged south, and as soon as Pip caught sight of the big bronze lion in the middle of the large road junction her pulse quickened with hope. A few minutes brought them inside the tall stone corridor covered with rich green creepers, and GI Joe and Philippe flew swiftly forward, following the grassy, disused train track leading into the black tunnel ahead. The birds raced through the veil of ivy into the gloom and landed beside the secret railway sleeper with the animals hurrying to the ground.

'Max!' Nancy knocked the sleeper swiftly three times, then once more, in a secret password, and her tail flicked impatiently as she repeated the sequence. 'Open up, you dodo!'

A moment later, Pip and the others heaved a sigh of relief as the timber trapdoor creaked ajar with Max's beady, black eyes shining from below.

'*Salut*, Nancy!' Max smiled fondly, levering the timber railway sleeper wide open with the pole and hopping out of the opening. Philippe struck a match as he rushed into the hole and Max's face suddenly fell, seeing Leo flopped listlessly in his beak. '*Oh non*, Leo! What happened?'

'There's no time for chit-chat, Max,' Nancy said, pushing Pip and the others into the opening. Looking up at the raven for a second, her eyes widened in horror. 'Max!' she yelled. 'LOOK OUT!'

The raven followed her gaze and gasped. Twelve hulking Goliath Rats were sprinting across the railway sleepers, straight towards them.

'Run!' Max cried, watching in horror as the Goliath Rats neared with their lips curling back from long yellow teeth. He shoved Nancy into the hole and she cursed as she fell upon Madame Fourcade's prickles. 'All of you, run as fast as you can!'

'Come with us!' the hedgehog yelled, ripping a match from the flip-top box and striking it against the ignition strip with a fizz.

'I'll be right behind you!' Max panted. 'Now go! GO!'

Madame Fourcade and Nancy rushed after the others. Max leaped into the secret passageway after them, throwing his full weight into the pole that held the trapdoor open. The railway sleeper slammed shut above his head, and he swiftly ignited another match to follow his friends. But a second later, the raven stopped dead, realizing he'd not heard the trapdoor click back into place, and he gasped, hearing the sound of scratching claws find the edges of the sleeper and slowly prise it open.

CHAPTER NINETEEN

THE GOLIATH RATS

'Where's Max?' Pip looked over her shoulder as she bounded between Philippe and GI Joe, pacing as fast as they could through the burrow.

'He's coming,' Madame Fourcade puffed behind the pigeon.

'Just keep going.' GI Joe urged Pip on. 'Don't look back!'

The flares billowed above Philippe and Madame Fourcade's head as they sprinted through the tunnel. A few panicked minutes brought them skidding to a halt at the wall of human skulls.

'I can hear the rats.' Nancy nervously shifted on her paws with Madame Fourcade, watching Philippe fumble with the bottom left skull's teeth and drop his match on the floor. As it snuffed out, the darkness closed around him and he whimpered with fear.

'Which tooth opens the door?' Pip cried, hearing the Goliath Rats' growls grow louder in the tunnel behind them and she pushed past the parrot to the skull that grinned at them in the gloom.

'Pull the lower left tooth!' Nancy rushed to Pip's side.

'Hurry!' Madame Fourcade winced, the flame of the match singeing her paw. 'I can't hold on to this torch for much longer!'

Pip found the tooth and pulled. A moment later, the hedgehog dropped the matchstick and a shaft of light shone in the darkness as Pip slowly dragged the skull's face outwards. Seeing her struggle, Philippe, Madame Fourcade and Nancy leaped to her aid and yanked the door wide open.

'Well done, *chérie*.' Madame Fourcade pushed Pip into the long secret passage freckled with fossils. 'We're almost there.'

Damp air filled their lungs as the animals rushed through the opening. Letting the door swing closed behind them, they dashed down the slope and followed the little lights, guiding them deep underground. A few breathless minutes brought them to the murky pool inside the large limestone chamber. Behind them, the roar of the Goliath

Rats grew louder as they chased the others inside.

'They've worked out the skulls! Quick!' Nancy said urgently. 'We've got to reach the ledge on the other side of the water before they see which way we've gone. The rats have to think we've taken the path of lights, otherwise our hideout is blown and it won't just be Leo's life that's in danger – it'll be the whole Parisian Resistance!'

'Let's get outta here!' GI Joe said as Pip scrambled on to his back with Madame Fourcade while Nancy climbed on to Philippe, and she'd barely grabbed the feathers behind his neck before he burst into the air.

With the sound of the approaching Goliath Rats screaming in their ears, the birds soared over the pool towards the small ledge on the opposite side of the cave. They were almost there when Nancy shrieked. A second later, the others gasped in horror as the white mouse lost her grip and plummeted into the pool with a small splash.

'Nancy!' Pip cried as Philippe landed on the ledge, closely followed by GI Joe.

The animals turned pale, watching Nancy splutter as she came to the surface. Knowing what lurked beneath her, her eyes widened with panic and she swam desperately towards Pip and Madame Fourcade, who were hurriedly dismounting from GI Joe.

'Don't wait for me!' Nancy ordered, nearing the ledge and seeing Philippe hesitate. 'Go and tell the raven guards the Goliath Rats are snapping at our heels! Now!'

'Go!' Pip added as she dived on to her stomach with Madame Fourcade and GI Joe. Together they reached Nancy's paw and dragged her to safety. 'Take Leo to the doctor! We'll catch up!'

Giving one last glance to his friends, the parrot disappeared into the dark corridor with Leo dangling from his beak. Pip watched the gloom consume him, hoping with all her heart that Leo was going to be all right. She'd only met him a matter of hours ago, yet she felt as though she'd known him forever. Just as she stepped to follow them a blood-curdling snarl snatched her breath from her lungs.

'UMBRELLA MOUSE!'

Pip's insides lurched with fear as she turned with GI Joe, Madame Fourcade and Nancy. Twelve Goliath Rats glared at them on the other side of the pool with gleaming red eyes.

'You cannot run from us any longer!' the biggest Goliath Rat spat, its muscular, auburn body rearing on its hind legs. 'Come with us now and we'll spare your friends' lives!'

'Don't listen to them.' Madame Fourcade wrapped her paw tightly round Pip and as her ear pressed against the hedgehog's chest, she heard Madame's heart drum. 'You cannot trust the enemy.'

'The Umbrella Mouse must pay for her crimes!' another rat cried.

'She is a murderer and a traitor to the regime!' the biggest rat growled. 'If she doesn't give herself up now, all of you will suffer!'

'You don't scare us, you mangey varmints!' Nancy glowered.

'She isn't going anywhere with you!' GI Joe stood in front of Pip and Madame Fourcade with his feathers ruffling furiously all over his body.

'GI Joe,' a soft female voice cooed in the familiar American accent that had once fooled them. Pip froze, recognizing it at once. 'I wondered if you survived the fire, honey. We searched for your body in the ashes.' She looked him up and down and smirked. 'You look like you should have died in the flames like your friends Hans and Léon.'

'Lucia . . .' GI Joe glowered at the white pigeon padding up to the Goliath Rats from the path behind. She smiled at the animals cowering across the pool of water and a deep growl rumbled in GI Joe's throat.

'I shall have my revenge, Pip,' the white pigeon snarled,

now speaking in her true German voice. 'You cannot get away with what you did at the Nacht und Nebel camp.'

'I'll never let you take her!' GI Joe flared.

'You can't stop me,' Lucia scoffed, 'and I'll crush anyone who tries, just like I killed your friends. And it's all your fault they are dead, Pip.'

Lucia's malice was like venom pulsing through Pip, Madame Fourcade and GI Joe's veins, and they edged closer to one another, feeling too weak with grief to stand alone.

'When will you learn?' Lucia's milky blue eyes glowed with pleasure, watching Pip and her friends suffer. 'A pathetic little orphan like you cannot beat us! This is your last chance. Come with us now or your friends will pay the price – starting with Madame Fourcade's hoglets!' The hedgehog's prickles stiffened against Pip's fur and Nancy and GI Joe drew sharp breaths. 'That's right, Madame.' Lucia chuckled. 'One of your precious allies has talked. It's only a matter of time before I find your little darlings and kill them too!'

'She's lying,' Madame Fourcade whispered. 'Nobody from Noah's Ark knows where they are.'

'A swallow visited your hideout three days ago, did it not?' Lucia asked, plumping her chest feathers with confidence.

Pip shivered. After they'd sabotaged the Tiger tanks with the Maquis, the Butcher Birds had impaled the remains of a bird with inky feathers on the bramble thorns. She suddenly realized they were exactly the same colour as Rémi the swallow's, who had visited Noah's Ark on the morning of the funeral. His visits were always brief and furtive, and Madame Fourcade had always shown more interest in his news than anything else, from the most dangerous sabotages to the best reports that the Allied armies were winning the war. Pip had always suspected he brought word of Madame Fourcade's hoglets, and now Lucia had found and killed him.

'You are mistaken.' Madame Fourcade replied calmly, but her body betrayed her words, and Pip hoped the white pigeon could not see the hedgehog tremble. 'I know no swallows.'

'My Butcher Birds had a little chat with one they caught in the forest,' Lucia went on, 'and he knew you and your hoglets very well, Madame. They are hidden inside an orphanage near Giverny, aren't they?'

'You're wrong.' Madame Fourcade gritted her teeth, but her eyes were glistening with tears.

'We'll soon see about that.' Lucia smirked. 'My largest troop of birds and rats are hunting them as we speak, but you have my word they will cease if Pip comes with me now.'

'You'll have to stop me first.' GI Joe said furiously,

opening his wings to fly, but Pip and Madame Fourcade leaped on him, shaking their heads, knowing he stood no chance against twelve Goliath Rats at once.

'By all means –' Lucia laughed, eyeing his thinner body up and down with the Goliath Rats salivating beside her – 'hand yourself to us on a plate! You always were reckless. That's what made you so easy to manipulate.'

Pip glared at the white pigeon with her little fists clenching and her blood thrumming with hatred. She loathed Lucia, the Goliath Rats, the Butcher Birds, the Axis and this vile and vicious war for murdering her parents, for killing her friends, for razing her home and for destroying the lives and spirits of those she loved. For Madame Fourcade to lose her hoglets this close to France's liberation after everything the hedgehog had risked and sacrificed for their sake was an intolerable cruelty Pip could not endure.

'Enough!' Pip cried, shaking with anger as she wriggled free of the hedgehog's embrace. 'You win! I'll come with you – just don't hurt anyone.'

'What are you doing?' GI Joe gasped as Nancy's mouth fell open in outrage.

'Stay where you are!' Madame Fourcade ordered. 'Lucia knows nothing!

'Go!' Pip cried, her mind whirring with an idea. 'I know what I'm doing!'

Madame Fourcade's prickles bristled. 'I'm not leaving you.'

'Trust me!' Pip whispered, and as they met each other's gaze her friends understood what she was doing. 'If you want me, Lucia –' she turned and faced the bird defiantly – 'then you'll have to come and get me!'

'And me!' Madame Fourcade cried.

'Me too!' GI Joe added.

'Count me in as well!' Nancy said defiantly, paws on hips.

'So if you want *us*,' Pip repeated, her pulse pounding in her ears, 'you'll have to come and get us!'

'As you wish,' Lucia cooed. With a flick of her wings the Goliath Rats plunged into the murky water and a sickly expression of satisfaction drew across her face as they glided powerfully across the pool.

'Please come, please come,' Pip whispered to herself, the rats nearing with every second. Her friends brushed against her fur and, together, they stood tall with racing hearts, watching a long tail fin emerge from the water.

'No!' Lucia shrieked, fluttering her wings in alarm.

The catfish's wide, gaping mouth lunged. Squealing in

panic, the rats feverishly tried to outswim it as it greedily darted through the water, rose up and swallowed them whole. Lucia let out a piercing cry of fury and launched into the air with her blue eyes bitterly narrowing at Pip on the other side of the chamber.

'Run!' GI Joe yelled, bursting open his wings.

'I'm not leaving you again, GI!' Pip replied firmly beside Madame Fourcade and Nancy.

The pigeons collided above the catfish as its vast, speckled green body rocketed out of the water and closed its monstrous, long-whiskered jaws around the last rat. As it disappeared below the surface with a splash of its tail, GI Joe took a sudden scratch to the eye and he tumbled through the air in pain. Quickly coming to his senses, he swiftly beat his wings and skimmed the pool with his tail feathers, and the catfish lurched out of the water with an empty snap of its mouth. Above, GI Joe charged into Lucia and together they somersaulted through the air and landed heavily on the ledge on the opposite side of the chamber.

Lucia was pinning GI Joe against the ground when a sudden gust of wind blew against Pip, Madame Fourcade and Nancy from the corridor to their right, and a moment later, they hurled themselves into little balls as a dark cloud of ravens stormed into the chamber and torpedoed into

Lucia in a whirlwind of black feathers.

'I'll get you for this, Pip!' Lucia screeched, tumbling from her perch on GI Joe's chest and fleeing up the secret passageway to the city above with the swarm of ebony birds swiftly pursuing her. 'You'll be sorry! I'll destroy you if it's last thing I do!'

'And don't come back!' Nancy shouted after her. She shook the water and her fury from her fur and looked down at Pip and Madame Fourcade, peeling each other from the floor. 'I think we deserve a stiff drink after the night we've had, don't you?'

CHAPTER TWENTY

HOUSE ARREST

The air was tense with exhaustion as Pip, Madame Fourcade and GI Joe entered the hideout and followed Nancy to the medical ward that was draped in Amélie's webs and gleamed with the glow of fireflies. The candlelit room felt even bigger now that most of the animals were fighting above ground, and as they passed what animals remained Pip noticed they were all droopy-eyed with fatigue. The hours without sleep seemed to hang from their fur and feathers. Pip glanced at her friends walking beside her, and saw they were all just as dishevelled, with Madame Fourcade looking most wretched of all.

Robert the bullfinch and Noor the kingfisher were still sending and receiving Morse code, and when Pip passed them scribbling messages the tight knot in her chest loosened a little, seeing the umbrella where she had left it on the ground beside them. Passing the tea stall made from a broken carriage clock turned on its side, they continued onwards under the vigilant gaze of the eight stony-faced rats guarding the stage in the centre of the room. The small, scruffy stray dog and ginger cat argued here, standing over the map of Paris that marked the Resistance's progress. Nancy hurried to them and they scowled, listening to how they had just encountered Lucia and the Goliath Rats. With one word from the dog, four of the burly rat guards marched to the entrance of the hideout.

'Umbrella Mouse!' the ginger cat cried, promptly moving to her with Nancy and the scruffy stray dog. Pip shuffled on her paws, wanting to find Leo and Philippe more than talk to the animals who were in charge of the Resistance's hideout. 'Nancy tells us you saved the Eiffel Tower and sabotaged the telephone lines inside the Nazis' military headquarters.' He energetically shook her little paw. 'Well done!'

'It was all of us –' Pip's cheeks flamed as she nodded to GI Joe, Madame Fourcade and Nancy – 'and Leo and Philippe.'

'We heard the white pigeon and her Goliath Rats attacked you,' the ginger cat added gravely, darting his gaze to Madame Fourcade.

Pip looked up at the hedgehog for comfort, but she was staring at the floor, her thoughts consumed by a fog of dismay.

'There's no need to worry, Madame.' The ginger cat's brow crinkled, seeing the defeat on Pip and Madame Fourcade's faces. 'Our hideout is the safest place for you. The raven guards will catch the white pigeon and make her sorry.'

'But Lucia got away.' Pip sighed, and the ginger cat's tail flicked angrily. 'She's still out there somewhere and she wants to harm everyone we hold dear.'

'The last we saw of her,' Nancy added firmly, 'she had an army of ravens on her tail. She'd be as mad as a cut snake to fight them, and as long as she's trapped she can't hurt anyone.'

'We'll find your hoglets,' Pip whispered to Madame Fourcade as GI Joe wrapped a wing round the hedgehog's shoulders. 'Let's go now.'

'It's not that simple.' Madame Fourcade shook her head and Pip's chest throbbed, seeing her so pale and haunted. 'Rémi the swallow may not have told Lucia exactly where my hoglets were, but he gave her enough intelligence to find them soon, and now that she knows where I am her Goliath Rats and Butcher Birds will be watching and waiting for me to go and find them. I could lead the enemy straight to my hoglets and anyone who is with me could be captured or killed too.' She paused and a solitary tear trickled down her cheek. 'But if I don't go I'm losing my chance to save them with every second that goes by. I feel as though I'm being buried alive. I don't know what to do.'

'Oh, Madame,' Nancy soothed as the scruffy stray dog and the ginger cat eyed one another with hardening jaws. She clicked her paw tips three times and urgently motioned for the squirrel sitting behind the carriage-clock tea stall to bring over some warm drinks. 'Our ravens will catch her and then none of us have anything to worry about,' she added as the squirrel arrived carrying a tray of three steaming thimbles. 'Drink this – it'll keep your strength up.' Nancy passed one each to Pip, Madame Fourcade and GI Joe, who all stared at the refreshments absentmindedly. 'Come on,' she bossed. 'Down the hatch!'

They did as they were told and slurped the thimbles dry.

'I'll take us to your hoglets now, Madame,' GI Joe offered, putting his empty cup back on the tray with the others. 'There's gotta be another exit into the city that the enemy doesn't know about. I bet Philippe and Leo will help us too. The bigger the team, the stronger the strike.

Lead the way to them, Pip!'

But Pip wasn't listening. Her eyes and ears were fixed on the scruffy stray dog and the ginger cat who were abruptly stepping away with Nancy and speaking quickly to one another in hushed tones. Pip swallowed, sensing none of them wanted Madame Fourcade to leave.

'Look, loves!' Nancy caught Pip's gaze and spoke in a cheery voice as she pointed to the far side of the chamber where Philippe sat. 'Leo's just over there.' Pip turned at once. 'He'll be wanting to see you.'

Pip raced ahead of Madame Fourcade and GI Joe as they weaved through the beds inside the medical ward, and a lump swelled in her throat when they found Leo lying under a handkerchief draped over an empty sardine can with blue fish printed on the side.

'How is he?' Pip whispered to Philippe, unable to take her eyes off Leo's little chest wrapped in one of Amélie's spider web bandages, but the parrot only drew a deep sigh. Pip bit her lip, fearing the worst.

'He'll be fine,' Amélie interrupted, squeezing between Pip and Madame Fourcade on the other side of the bed. She picked up Leo's wrist in one of her tarsi and waited a moment, before patting it and resting it by his side again. 'Nice, slow, strong pulse,' she said, jotting something on a clipboard made from a metal bottle top. 'The shock is subsiding.'

'Oh, Doctor!' Leo croaked, and Pip beamed with her friends. 'You could have let her worry about me for a little longer!'

'If you had kept your mouth shut and pretended to be asleep like I said –' Philippe chuckled – 'she would've believed you.'

'*Si*, I know,' Leo said, gazing up at his friends, 'but I wanted to see you all again.'

'Leo is bashed and bruised, but it's nothing a good rest and a hearty meal can't fix.' Amélie's eight eyes travelled over Pip and the others. 'You should all try to do the same.'

She scuttled away to attend to other patients in nearby beds and Leo's brow furrowed, seeing the devastation lining the faces of his friends.

'*Topolina*,' Leo said, wincing a little as he lifted his head off his pillow made from a pink velvet pincushion. 'What's happened?'

Pip's eyes brimmed with tears as she recounted their confrontation with Lucia and the Goliath Rats. Leo and Philippe gaped in alarm at hearing that Madame Fourcade's hoglets were in peril, and they instantly vowed to help get them back in whatever ways they could.

The animals in the chamber were suddenly startled by the troop of ravens returning inside the Resistance's hideout in a flurry of squawks and clattering wings. A pair of them raced Max's limp body to the medical ward and Amélie and the fireflies rushed to his aid, while the rest of the birds hurried to Nancy, the scruffy stray dog and the ginger cat.

'*What?*' Nancy roared, and the fury in her voice made all whiskers droop in the room. 'If the white pigeon escaped, then the enemy knows where our hideout is!'

'If we're attacked and captured here –' Madame Fourcade's eyes widened with fear – 'my hoglets are doomed.'

Pip locked eyes with GI Joe, and his feathers ruffled with unease.

'Nancy, we need to move the hideout before we're besieged,' Madame Fourcade said, turning from Leo's bedside and marching towards the middle of the room.

'So you can abandon us and find your hoglets, Madame?' Nancy snapped, whipping her head round to her.

Madame Fourcade ignored her tone and stood tall under her stare. 'My hoglets are my business, not—'

'No,' Nancy corrected, 'they are everyone else's in this room, Madame! That dastardly white pigeon has laid a trap for you, knowing a mother will protect her young at all costs. You will give the enemy everything they want to save your hoglets' lives.'

'I would never!' Madame Fourcade bristled, but doubt soon made her stutter, 'I . . . I swear it! I promise I won't—'

'Let me make myself clear,' Nancy said firmly. 'If you leave, you are endangering not only yourself *and* your hoglets, but also the entire Resistance. You know too much, Madame. In an interrogation, you could be our undoing when our liberation rests on keeping our secrets safe. The enemy greatly outnumbers us in weapons, and our ammunition is running out. The Allied armies have not arrived and victory is uncertain. The uprising could fail at any moment. Your judgement is impaired by exhaustion and fear. You and your friends cannot be trusted until Paris is free.'

'But if we are attacked or captured or worse,' Pip cried, 'then we don't have a chance of rescuing her hoglets!'

'It's a sacrifice I wish we did not have to make,' Nancy said sadly, and the blood instantly drained from Madame Fourcade's face, 'but many more lives will be lost if you talk, Madame. We cannot lose Paris to the invaders again. As Madame Fourcade said herself, the white pigeon has not found her hoglets yet. The Milice are already being crushed like fleas as the human Allied army advances—'

'But if we stay here, we could all be captured!' GI Joe added, rushing to Madame Fourcade's side. 'We'll have fewer fighters on the ground to fight the enemy. We must at least move somewhere else inside the catacombs.'

'And get lost in more than a hundred miles of underground quarries?' Nancy scoffed. '*And* let our members returning from battle be trapped by the enemy inside our own hideout? Never!' she cried, her hazel eyes darting to the raven guards. 'Ravens! Go and guard the entrance in the abandoned railway tunnel at once and kill any Goliath Rat or white pigeon on sight.'

'But what if they're overrun like Max?' Pip frowned as the birds disappeared from the chamber.

'Fifty ravens cannot be overpowered.'

Madame Fourcade scowled. 'Then you're risking everyone's lives on the arrival and victory of the human Allied armies.'

'*All* our lives depend on that!' Nancy spat as Madame Fourcade suddenly swayed to the right. GI Joe propped her up and stumbled himself. At the same moment, Pip also felt faint, and Madame Fourcade and GI Joe paused, then stared at the squirrel behind the tea stall with a gasp of alarm.

'You've drugged us!' Madame Fourcade cried out, aghast. 'You ruthless . . . How could you . . .'

'It's the only way I can guarantee our safety,' Nancy interrupted. 'If you escaped the Nacht und Nebel camp, you'll try to break out of here too. You and your group are under my authority now and I forbid any of you to leave! Guards!' The white mouse clapped her paws together and at once the rats standing at the four corners of the stage turned their heads to her. 'Take the Umbrella Mouse and her friends to the beds beyond the medical ward and do not let them out of your sight.'

'You can't make us stay here against our will.' Pip shook her head in disbelief as the guards pointed their spears at Madame Fourcade and GI Joe.

'Please,' Madame Fourcade pleaded as she and GI Joe were prodded across the chamber towards the dormitory. 'My hoglets are in danger. They need me!'

'Keeping you under my watch is the only way I can stop you and your friends being caught and interrogated, Madame.' Nancy's face softened as a third guard neared Pip, trying her hardest to fight the effects of the drug by stubbornly gripping Leo's bedside with her paws. He squeezed one of her paws in his and his warmth made her feel stronger. 'The rats and ravens are the finest guards in

France – no other place is safer for you and your hoglets now. By staying here, you cannot lead the enemy to them.'

Pip looked around at all her friends submitting to Nancy's will and her heart sank with defeat.

'Rest well, little one,' Nancy added as Pip hung her head and followed Madame Fourcade and GI Joe, 'and I hope the human Allied armies will come to Paris's aid soon.'

Under the watchful eyes of the guards, Pip clambered inside a small, cream tin with the word *Pastilles* printed in red between green illustrations of curling leaves. Sinking into a thick pile of fluffy feathers, she covered herself with an old checked handkerchief draped upon it, and watched Madame Fourcade clamber into the neighbouring bed made from a fraying wicker breadbasket, and curl up into a ball. A lump swelled in Pip's throat, seeing the hedgehog's fear and despair ripple across her quills. Unable to bear the thought of her being alone, Pip whipped off her blanket and hurried to her. Climbing into Madame Fourcade's bed, Pip nestled against her prickles and the hedgehog's cold paw reached out for hers. Pip drew it into her chest with tears filling her eyes, and promised herself she would defy Nancy and stay awake for her friend. But, within a few minutes, both the hedgehog and the little mouse drifted into a cold, dark sleep.

In the hours before dawn, high above the Resistance's hideout in the catacombs, the great bell of Notre-Dame swung on its yoke for the first time in four years of occupation. Booming into the night, hope spread with every chime as, one by one, all the churches joined in the refrain, joyously ringing in a citywide symphony under the stars.

The citizens of Paris flung open their windows and doors and giddily dashed into the streets to hear them drown out the sounds of gunfire. At the same time, the animals barked and cawed and leaped into the air with their tails wagging and their hearts singing. The human Allied army had finally arrived.

Pip woke groggily, feeling an urgent shake of her shoulder. Blinking nervously, her eyes focused on Madame Fourcade, squatting at the side of the bed, and a sharp bite of shame gnawed at her as she realized she'd failed to stay awake for her.

'What's going on?' Pip asked, darting her eyes about her, and she brightened as she spied Leo looking more himself, standing behind Madame Fourcade with GI Joe and Philippe. Pip's heart sank, staring into the hedgehog's face. She'd never seen her look so wretched with anxiety.

'The human Allied army arrived last night!' Leo grinned with Philippe.

'The German General von Choltitz has just surrendered,' Madame Fourcade added earnestly. 'The Allies and the Resistance fought the enemy all day. Get up, *chérie*, we must get out of here and find my hoglets.'

'I've slept *all day*?' Pip gaped as Madame Fourcade helped her to the floor. 'Why didn't you wake me?'

'There was no point,' the hedgehog replied. 'The sleeping draught which that Nancy gave us made us dead to the world, and her guards have been like our shadows up until now. Come on, we need to get your umbrella and then we cannot stay a moment longer. I don't trust Nancy. She can't keep us here now, but she could find a reason for us to stay. She's distracted by the celebrations – we must go now!'

'Have Lucia or the Goliath Rats tried to come back?'

Pip swallowed as they walked briskly towards the middle of the chamber, where the large crowd of Resistance animals had returned from their sabotage missions and were now mingling together around the stage.

GI Joe shook his head. 'There's been no sign of them, liddle lady. The ravens guarding the entrance at the abandoned railway track haven't seen them, nor have the other fighters who've come back into the catacombs that way.'

'The Axis and the Milice are running back to Berlin with their tails between their legs!' Leo added.

Pip tried to smile in reply, but doubt hummed inside her. Lucia's quest for vengeance wouldn't let her retreat. It would make her stay, and as she glanced at Madame Fourcade biting her lip with worry, she knew the hedgehog was thinking the same.

The air in the room was electric as Pip and her friends weaved through the crowded throng of Resistance animals to the other side of the chamber, where Robert the bullfinch and Noor the kingfisher were still sending and receiving Morse code beside the umbrella. Every face Pip gazed up at was smiling and muttering excitedly; some were bandaged and bruised while others were leaning on crutches, but all of them – even the stone-faced rat and raven guards –

had the same joyful expression as they chattered to their comrades. Madame Fourcade shared a secretive nod with Robert the bullfinch as they arrived beside him, and GI Joe and Philippe carried the umbrella away under their wings.

Behind them, two rabbits rolled a bottle of champagne over the rugged, limestone floor. As they neared the stage in the middle of the room, four burly rat guards joined them, unravelling wire and gold foil, and they groaned with effort as they turned the cork, bulging out of its neck.

'Careful!' Nancy yelled across the room. 'All that bumping across the ground will make it—'

A loud *POP* sounded and the Resistance animals squealed with joy as they suddenly found themselves dripping with bubbling French wine.

Unknown to them, Madame Fourcade had swiftly led Pip and the others away.

CHAPTER TWENTY-ONE

THE ORPHANAGE

Deep beneath the feet of the Parisian men and women revelling with the Allied armies that had delivered them from the tyranny of Nazi rule, Pip, Madame Fourcade, Leo, GI Joe, Philippe and the umbrella hurried through the underground limestone quarries and arrived in the trampled flower bed inside the Luxembourg Gardens. Hurrying north-west through the bright afternoon skies, their hearts burst at the sights and sounds of riotous celebration in the city below.

Men, women and children unfurled in every direction as they cheered for the victorious armies. The birds swooped above the jubilant throng, waving French, American, British and USSR flags and pointing their fingers to the sky in V-signs. Many sang the French national anthem while others threw flowers or leaped upon the soldiers to kiss their cheeks. More watched from rooftops and windows, and Pip giggled, spying an elderly woman clutching a poodle dressed in the same blue, white and red stripes as the tricolour billowing from her balcony in the hot summer breeze.

'This is what freedom looks like,' Madame Fourcade said behind Pip, straddling GI Joe carrying the umbrella in his talons with Philippe, soaring over the sea of people below.

As a London mouse in unoccupied Britain, Pip had never known what it meant to be overpowered by another country. Now watching the men and women rejoicing together, she realized how lucky she'd been.

'How long will it be until everybody is free?' she asked, eyes darting over the triumphant crowd passing beneath them.

'The war isn't over in France yet,' Madame Fourcade replied. 'Even after the success of the advance through Normandy and the liberation of Paris, the invader still holds Atlantic positions to the west and it will take time for the Allies to complete the invasion of the south and east.' Pip sighed, whiskers drooping on her cheeks. 'I know it feels like it will never end, *chérie*,' the hedgehog continued softly, 'but it won't be long before we push the enemy all the way back to Berlin.'

'She's right,' Leo added from Philippe's back, where the parrot was flapping his wings beside them. 'The human Allied army will be gathering and heading towards the Rhine soon.'

'But they gotta strike fast,' GI Joe said gravely. 'They can't let the Axis armies regroup and regain their strength.'

Gunfire suddenly erupted below and the throng of people flung themselves flat on the ground. Panicked cries rang out as men and women covered their heads, and mothers and fathers shielded their children.

'Snipers!' GI Joe cried, swiftly swerving with Philippe.

'I thought they had surrendered!' Pip gasped at the smoke rising from a building to their left, and Allied soldiers and Resistance fighters on the ground instantly aimed their rifles at its open windows. Pip's hackles rose. Even in times of triumph nobody was safe.

'They did!' Leo flinched with the others as bullets ripped the air open.

'GI, Philippe – fly as fast as you can!' Madame Fourcade cried as they looked over their shoulders at the gunfight, abruptly quietening, and the men and women tentatively peeled their bodies off the ground and continued celebrating. 'We have to get to my hoglets before anything happens to them!'

Storming over the rooftops, GI Joe and Philippe followed Madame Fourcade's directions north-west. They soared towards the sun creeping to the horizon for the rest of the day, leaving the city behind them, and tracked the familiar shimmer of the Seine, which snaked through yellow and green fields.

The clouds were gleaming with the first silvers of twilight when Pip recognized the woodlands and willow trees where they'd said farewell to Henri with the seagulls. She hoped they knew the battle for Paris had been won. Each act of resistance all over Normandy had contributed to the Allied success, and every fighter, big or small, animal or human, deserved to be proud.

Madame Fourcade pointed them towards a small town, separated from its northern outskirts by the River Seine. Its buildings were jagged and torn by recent bombing raids, but as the birds descended they breathed easier, spying the domed helmets and khaki uniforms of the Allied army on its shorelines. In the heat of the summer evening, many of the men worked bare chested, assembling decking over a long line of large empty canoes, bobbing across the water.

'Look!' Pip beamed, pointing her paw to a completed floating bridge. A group of soldiers were walking across it and two Alsatians bounded ahead of the men.

'Who are they?' Leo asked, ears pricking as they stared at the dogs below.

'Brian and Bing – the sky-dogs!' Pip replied. 'They parachute with army platoons and protect the men on the ground. We met them on the way to Paris.'

The pigeon and the parrot swooped to fly alongside the Alsatians and Pip called out their names.

'Hello!' Bing leaped into the air with a wagging tail. 'How was Paris, Pip?'

'Sorry we couldn't join you –' Brian smiled with his long pink tongue dangling out of his mouth – 'but we hear our French and Americans friends arrived.'

'They sure did,' GI Joe cooed.

'And now Paris is liberated!' Pip cried.

Bing continued trotting along with his head held high. 'We're heading east through France and Belgium to do the same.'

'Once we've rested overnight with our men,' Brian added. 'We had some trouble securing this part of the river, but the humans in the Resistance helped us, sabotaging that road bridge over there and liberating the southern part of the town before we arrived.'

Brian gestured with his nose to a tall overpass crossing

the water to the left. One of its six thick concrete legs had been blown away, destroying the road above.

'Look at that!' a soldier suddenly gasped behind them, pointing to the bizarre group of animals carrying an umbrella in the air beside the dogs.

'You best be off,' Bing said.

'Hurry, GI Joe, Philippe,' Madame Fourcade urged as the birds climbed into the air again. 'We don't have any time to waste!'

The men murmured in astonishment at the strange sight of an African Grey parrot and a pigeon swiftly swerving an umbrella to the left across the river towards the fringes of the town where a secluded house overlooked the water.

The sky was ablaze with sunset when they reached the orphanage upon the hill, surrounded by tall oaks and fir trees looming above the riverbank. The birds landed at the edge of a grassy glade and a chill rippled over Pip's fur, as if a cool breeze floated on the wind, but not a single leaf stirred in the dense evening air.

'Are you sure this is the right place, Madame?' GI Joe whispered, amber eyes darting around the glass windows that glared with the scarlet clouds above. The animals cocked their ears. An eerie stillness enveloped the clearing.

No birds tweeted; no crickets cheeped. Even the trees stood silently as though trying not to be heard. 'I don't think there are any orphans here.'

'The children must be on an excursion or may have been evacuated from the recent battle.' Madame Fourcade's voice was unconvincingly cheery, and Pip and the others glanced at one another uneasily. 'The swallows and my little hoglets wouldn't have left their hiding place, in any case.' She patted GI Joe's wings, signalling him and the parrot to carry the animals and the umbrella inside. 'Let's go.'

The birds launched into the air and flew to the back of the building where a large redbrick stable stood in a meadow of long, parched grass, dotted with wilted sunflowers. They landed and the mice and hedgehog dismounted, Madame Fourcade's paws trembling as she pushed aside a large rusty grate leaning against the lowest bricks of the barn. Revealing a hole the size of a large shoebox, the hedgehog scurried inside, followed by GI Joe, then Philippe, carrying the umbrella tucked under their wings. Pip's heart filled with dread as she padded forward with Leo, flattening his ears beside her.

The animals padded into the barn towards an open stable door that framed the sunset-drenched glade beyond and softly illuminated an empty hay manger fixed to the wall above an aged wooden floor, scattered with feathers and blades of straw.

'There used to be chickens here . . .' Madame Fourcade's voice wavered, and she rushed to a row of nesting boxes on the ground to the right. Feverishly scrabbling at the bedding in the middle alcove, she uncovered a secret burrow beneath and slipped her head inside.

Seconds passed, as if in slow motion, and Pip didn't dare look at the others shifting nervously on their paws and claws. With her throat tightening, she stared at a spider's web spiralling from the timber wall and her thoughts drifted to Amélie. Her silk had treated so many, but Pip knew some wounds never fully healed and, clenching her little paws into fists, she willed for Madame Fourcade to find her hoglets inside.

Madame Fourcade reappeared a moment later, panic shaking her quills. 'They're not here.' Her words struck Pip and the others like a blow to the chest and their eyes glistened with sadness, seeing the agony seizing the hedgehog's face. 'Swallows!' Madame Fourcade cried, her gaze desperately spinning round the eaves of the stable where four barren nests clung to each corner of the barn. 'Swallows! Please answer me! Where are you?'

A cold silence replied and then they saw them. On

the far side of the barn, near the open stable door, two birds with the same inky-coloured wings and forked tails that Pip had seen before in the forest were slumped on the ground. Their necks were collapsed and their wings were splayed unevenly. Pip covered her mouth with her paws, realizing their feathers were plucked and torn.

'Swallows!' Madame Fourcade yelled, skittering towards them, but no answer could come.

Pip went to her, not knowing what to say or do. Behind them, GI Joe, Leo and Philippe bowed their heads.

'Christian! Béatrice!' Madame Fourcade sobbed, paws bunching up at her prickly forehead in despair. 'Please! I can't have lost you now. Not after everything . . . not when we're so close to the end.'

Madame Fourcade whimpered and Pip took her paw in her own and squeezed it in the same way the hedgehog had done so many times for her. As their eyes met, Madame Fourcade's face crumpled with sorrow and Pip flung her arms round her. Madame had ached from being separated from her young and every moment she'd spent fighting the war with Noah's Ark was so that her hoglets could grow up in a world free of tyranny and cruelty. But now they were gone, and tears brimmed as Pip thought of how much the hedgehog had done for her since they had met. She would do anything to take her pain away. She just wished she knew how.

GI Joe, Leo and Philippe edged closer and wrapped their paws and feathers around them. Their quiet, collective warmth steadied Pip and Madame Fourcade, who wept into Pip's shoulder.

'*Mon dieu*,' Philippe suddenly said under his breath.

'Holy cow!' GI Joe squawked, lifting his head towards the scratching and shuffling sounds to their right. 'Madame! Pip! You're not gonna believe it!'

Pip and Madame Fourcade sniffed as they untangled themselves from their grip and looked into their friends' astonished expressions. A large shard of cracked wood was shifting in the floor by the wall.

'Over there!' Leo pointed his paw to two little prickly faces peeking out from beneath the wood. 'Look!'

The bigger one blinked – 'Mama?' – and Madame Fourcade's mouth fell open as she turned to her son.

'Mama!' her daughter cried.

Both hoglets scrambled out of their hiding place and jumped into their mother's open arms. Covering one another in hugs and kisses, joyful laughter filled the stable, and Pip and her friends beamed with relief that hope was not lost. Watching Madame Fourcade reunite with her

hoglets, the end of the war seemed closer, the possibility of the future was brighter and, for the first time, Pip allowed herself a rush of excitement, imagining herself inside the umbrella museum in Gignese.

'*Mon coeur*,' Madame Fourcade said at last, 'what happened to the chickens and the swallows and where are the humans in the orphanage?' Christian and Béatrice's faces fell, catching sight of the remains of the two birds who had cared for them for so long. 'It's all right,' Madame Fourcade said softly, guiding their gazes away from the swallows by gently turning them round. 'Quickly, tell me what you saw.'

'Late last night –' Christian stared at the floor – 'Axis soldiers arrived in trucks and took all the humans in the house away.'

'And they snatched the chickens,' Béatrice whimpered. 'It was horrible, Mama. All of them were screaming.' Madame Fourcade hushed her daughter and drew her into her furry chest. Pip remembered her mother doing the same for her when she was upset, and sighed sadly, wishing she could feel her embrace again.

'As soon as they drove away, the swallows hurried us under this floorboard. It wasn't long before we heard more voices and we lifted the board just a little to see what was happening. Huge rats and a swarm of grey birds with black markings around their eyes had surrounded the swallows over there.' Christian pointed to the stable door as his sister wept beside him. 'They were looking for you, Mama. They said Rémi told them about the orphanage, but the rest of the swallows pretended they didn't know who he was.'

'Then they killed them,' Béatrice added, sniffing.

'Where did those grey birds go, *mon coeur*?' Madame Fourcade asked urgently, crouching low in a desperate bid to make them feel safer. 'Have you seen them again? Are they still here?'

Pip's heart thudded in her ears and the animals' breath grew shallow, seeing fear snatch the voices from the hoglets' throats.

'I . . . I don't know, Mama,' Christian replied at last. 'We've been—'

At that moment, countless wings drummed outside the barn, and Pip and her friends froze as a chilling voice cried out in the gathering gloom.

'Oh, little Miss Umbrella Mouse!' Lucia sang, as though they were old friends playing a game. 'Come out, come out, wherever you are! We know you're in there!'

'*Mon dieu*,' Madame Fourcade whispered, drawing her hoglets close as claws scratched the roof over their heads. 'We're trapped!'

'We can outfly those worms,' GI Joe said firmly. 'Put your hoglets on my back and let's get out of here!'

'Come on!' Leo frowned at Pip, standing rooted to the ground as the others hurried on to the birds.

Pip hesitated, her mind racing. 'If they catch us, all of us will fall. It's me they want, not you.'

'No, *chérie*.' Madame Fourcade shook her head. 'You are a symbol of resistance in the fight against evil. They'll make an example of you and show you no mercy. You *must* come with us now!'

'No!' Pip cried, her heart pounding with an idea. The thoughts rushing through her head terrified her, but Lucia had to be stopped, and there was only one way she knew how. 'Two mice, three hedgehogs and the umbrella will be too heavy. The risk of capture is too high.'

'No, liddle lady,' GI Joe cooed, 'we can outfly—'

'Listen to me!' Pip's hackles rose. 'We're out of time! All of you, hide under that floorboard now! I'll give myself up and you need to follow wherever they take me. Then you need to split up.' She whipped her head to the parrot carrying Leo, who was staring at her incredulously. 'Philippe, go into the town and shout for Brian and Bing. Bernard Booth instructed them to help us and they'll come to our aid when they find out what's happened.' She turned to the pigeon and the hedgehogs next. 'GI Joe, fly as fast as you can to the seagull colony in the willow tree. They're the only creatures we know who have beaten the Butcher Birds and Lucia before. I hope you'll be able to find me . . .' The possibility of never seeing them again stole her breath from her lungs for a moment. 'So go!' she cried. 'Now!'

'But, *chér*—' Madame Fourcade pleaded.

'I'm begging you! Hide!' Pip trembled, hearing the Butcher Birds' shrieks as they neared the open stable door. 'Before it's too late!'

Knowing Pip was right, her friends raced into the gap in the floorboard from which the hoglets had emerged, and shuffled the large shard of wood over their heads as quickly as they could. It slotted back into place as if they'd never been there, and Pip stepped beside her umbrella with her blood thundering through her veins.

A flurry of wings entered the barn and Pip closed her eyes to steady the terror bellowing inside her. Picturing the smiling faces of Mama, Papa, Hans, Léon and Henri, she felt stronger, imagining they were standing with her in the shadows. A moment later, a gust of wind blew about her whiskers and she swallowed, knowing Lucia and the Butcher Birds had arrived.

'All alone with your umbrella, Pip?' Lucia sneered, landing directly in front of her. Pip met the white pigeon's milky-blue glare and held her arms close to her body to stop them from shaking. 'Where have your friends flown off to?'

'I'll never tell you.' Pip glowered, trying to ignore the Butcher Birds edging closer from all sides with their black hooked beaks glinting in the shadows.

'I doubt that,' the white pigeon scoffed. 'We have ways of making you talk.' She cocked her head towards her army of shrikes. 'Take her and the umbrella into the house, and turn this barn upside down for the others.'

The Butcher Birds burst into the air and swirled about the stable in a dark cloud, pecking at the eaves above and clawing at the planks below. Feeling sick with fear for her friends, Pip clutched the umbrella to steady her quaking, and a moment later, hearing the shrikes screech in frustration at finding no trace of them, the churn in her stomach eased.

'Lift your paws above your head!' a Butcher Bird snarled, hovering over her with its black-tipped wings brushing her fur. Pip hugged the umbrella tighter, knowing she couldn't stop them from taking it, but she couldn't give it up without a fight. In the next moment, another shrike torpedoed into her from behind and she landed flat on her stomach with outstretched paws. Her face slammed against the rough wooden floor and she winced in pain as her cheek was snagged with splinters.

Two Butcher Birds seized her wrists in their talons and Pip dangled helplessly in the air, high above her friends hidden below the ground.

CHAPTER TWENTY-TWO

PIP'S SACRIFICE

Darkness had fallen when Lucia led her troop of shrikes into the abandoned house through the open front door, left ajar by the orphans and their carers the night before. They passed through a wide corridor decorated with drawings of flowers and bright landscapes, and the rooms inside were quiet, as if grieving for the chatter of children.

The birds glided into an empty assembly hall overlooked by four tall French doors looming over a parquet floor, illuminated by the cold glow of the moon rising through the thin windowpanes.

As the shrikes whirled around the room, they dropped Pip from above and she tumbled heavily across the floor. Wincing, she took a deep breath to steady her terror and stood to face Lucia and the Butcher Birds, who crowded round her and the umbrella in a circle.

'At last.' Lucia smiled as thirty Goliath Rats scuttled out of the shadows to join them. 'The Umbrella Mouse: *the myth, the flame of hope, the heart of the Resistance* – pah!' She spat as if the words scorched her mouth. 'The rebellion is deluded. Now the story of your downfall will spread and every animal will despise you for your deceit.'

'Whatever you do to me,' Pip said, holding her little head high but aching with fear inside, 'the Resistance will never stop fighting you.'

'They will when they know what a fraud you are.' Lucia's eyes narrowed bitterly. 'You're not on a mission to free Europe from "the Nazi snare". You're on a desperate quest not to be alone. You're a grief-stricken orphan, yearning for a family, unable to let go of your umbrella and your past. Noah's Ark knows this – it's what Madame Fourcade used to manipulate you right from the start.'

'You're lying.' Pip frowned. 'Madame Fourcade and Noah's Ark are my friends and the umbrella is my *future*, not just my past.'

'You don't honestly believe you ever had a chance of taking it to Northern Italy, do you?' Lucia scoffed. 'Madame Fourcade only goes along with it because she knows you need her help getting there. But you never will.

She can't have you leaving Noah's Ark now she's made you a symbol of the rebellion. She doesn't love you, Pip,' the white pigeon cooed softly, watching Pip's eyes fill with tears. 'None of them do. They've used you to distract the Resistance from a failing battle that they are destined to lose.'

'I'll never believe anything you say,' Pip said through gritted teeth, trying not to let Lucia's words in, but they twisted painfully in her chest. She'd sacrificed finding her mother's family in Italy to help Noah's Ark win the war that had killed her parents. The thought never crossed her mind that Madame Fourcade could be using her. It couldn't be true. 'Madame Fourcade and Noah's Ark are my family.'

'Your need to be loved makes you weak.' Lucia sighed, her expression softening, moving towards Pip and reaching out her wing to the little mouse's shoulder. 'When will you learn that true freedom comes from being alone? Opening your heart gives others power. Being an orphan is a gift – having nobody makes us stronger! Join me and I'll teach you how to harness its force.'

Lucia eyes gleamed with earnest and Pip's insides squirmed. Hans and Léon had warned her how evil preyed upon those who had suffered the most and, for a moment, Pip felt sorry for Lucia. If she was hand-reared by a Nazi pigeon handler like GI Joe thought, she never stood a chance. Her heart and her mind would have been lost from birth. She knew Lucia. Remorse would never come.

'It's your last hope for survival, Pip,' Lucia continued. 'Only the Axis can deliver you and your umbrella to the museum in our territory in Northern Italy. If you cooperate and tell us everything you know about Churchill's Secret Animal Army and the Resistance, we can take you there tomorrow.'

'I'll never join you or tell you anything about my friends!' Pip cried out in outrage. '*A secret is only a secret if it remains unspoken!*'

'Churchill's Secret Animal Army motto cannot save you now.' Lucia's eyes flashed with impatience. 'No one but us can free the world from oppression, and we will triumph.'

'You're wrong,' Pip said firmly, knowing what she'd seen and heard in Paris. 'The Allies are winning the war. They've liberated Paris and they're advancing towards Germany from the north, west and south.'

'That's what we want you to think.' Lucia plumped her chest feathers with self-satisfaction. 'Our troops are regrouping and preparing for an attack that the Allied armies cannot withstand. You will perish too if you stay on the wrong side. No one, especially an ordinary little mouse kitten like you, can undermine the might of the Nazi regime and live. This is your last chance. Join us,' the white pigeon snarled, 'or die.'

'I'm not scared of you, Lucia –' Pip met the white pigeon's cold, blue stare and felt a calm confidence hum through her body – 'because I know everything you've told me is a lie. Being an orphan doesn't mean I'm alone – I carry everyone I have lost with me wherever I go.'

'How trite.' Lucia sniggered with her army of Butcher Birds and Goliath Rats, and spittle spewed from their beaks and mouths. 'Does that mean your friends Hans and Léon are with us now?'

Pip felt a sharp bite of grief, seeing the same flash of Hans and Léon's last moments that had haunted her every day since she had broken Madame Fourcade and the others free from the Nacht und Nebel camp. But this time she pushed the image away and chose to remember how they made her feel instead, and at once warmth spread across her chest. She knew she could never bring them back, but their spirits would live on if Pip never gave up their fight.

'Opening your heart to others isn't weak either – it's *brave*,' she continued defiantly, trying not to listen to the cruel jibes echoing around the room. 'And having a family means fighting for those you love no matter what. That's why I stay with Noah's Ark and Madame Fourcade. We've all made sacrifices so that the future will be safe from hatred and tyranny – yet you think the Nazi regime has set you free. *You're* the one who is deluded, Lucia, *not* the Resistance.'

'Watch your mouth,' Lucia hissed, and silence rippled over the Butcher Birds and Goliath Rats at once. 'Or you will be sorry.'

'You've given up on the world because you cannot forgive it for making you an orphan and a misfit who doesn't belong.' Pip's heart drummed with daring, ignoring Lucia's threat, and the white pigeon's feathers ruffled furiously all over her body. 'You want revenge for your suffering and that's exactly what the Nazis have used to manipulate *you*. Now you're trapped inside Hitler's iron fist and all of you are going to be crushed by a madman. *You* need to change sides if you're going to survive – not me.'

'What do you know of pain and sacrifice?' Lucia sneered. 'You've had someone protecting you every step of the way. But there's no one to help you now . . .' Lucia stepped forward with the Butcher Birds and the Goliath Rats, who bared their teeth as they closed in around Pip and the umbrella. 'If you won't give us the information we want, you will be punished. Do you know what the humans do in France? They chop their enemies' heads off with the guillotine. But somehow –' Lucia paused, cocking her head in thought, and a sinister smile drew across her beak – 'I don't think that frightens you enough.'

'There's nothing you can do to make me betray my friends,' Pip snapped. She would never reveal anything that could harm them, no matter what Lucia did to her.

'Are you sure?' Lucia's milky-blue gaze darted to the umbrella. A rush of panic surged through Pip as the Butcher Birds and the Goliath Rats cackled with glee. Seeing Pip's eyes widen with fear, the white pigeon loomed over her and tut-tutted. 'What would your parents think of you now? Throwing away your ancestral family umbrella for the sake of a manipulative hedgehog and her band of swindling animals? If anything happens to it, you'll be betraying your parents' last wish and failing every umbrella mouse before you.'

Pip couldn't speak, her mind flooding with memories of curling up with Mama and Papa in their nest hidden deep inside the umbrella canopy, and wrapping her tail round its metal ribs to watch customers come and go from the umbrella shop in London. Nothing could describe how much she missed the sound of Mama and Papa's voices or the brush of their fur against hers, and she would do anything to go back and listen to Papa's stories and tickle her whiskers with Mama's one last time. The umbrella was the only thing she had left of them and the thought of losing it felt as terrifying as losing her own life. But, as blood rang in her ears, she was sure that all Mama and Papa had ever really wanted was for her to be safe in a world without the menace of war. After everything she had learned since she'd lost her parents in the bomb blast in London, she knew she could survive without the umbrella because the life she'd had inside it would live in her memories forever, just like everyone else she had lost.

'For the last time,' Lucia snarled, 'tell me everything you know about Churchill's Secret Animal Army and the Resistance or my Butcher Birds and Goliath Rats will destroy your family home!'

Pip shuffled nervously on her paws.

'Answer me!' Lucia snapped.

Dread crushed the breath in Pip's chest. Her friends were too late. She'd gambled the umbrella on them finding help in time and now her last shred of Mama and Papa had met its end. With her heart splintering, Pip turned away from it, and bile rushed up her throat at the sound of gnashing teeth and slashing claws destroying everything she'd ever known.

But as she began to sob, with grief wracking her little body, suddenly the sound of smashing glass blasted through the assembly room and Pip whipped her head over her shoulder.

'NO!' Lucia screeched in horror, her beak falling open in disbelief as a storm of seagulls torpedoed through the large windowpanes.

Lucia and the shrikes leaped into the air and the birds spiralled above Pip's head in a bitter brawl of beaks and claws. Before the shattered glass scattered across the floor, galloping hooves and thudding paws thundered to the right and Pip's insides soared, seeing Henri charge into the assembly room with the Maquis' wolves, Gabriel and Madeleine by his side.

The stag trampled and stamped while the wolves tore through the hall, ploughing through the Goliath Rats on the ground with their open jaws. But some of the rats were fast, and they jumped, their long, yellow teeth and nails bared for blood. A moment later, Henri, Madeleine and Gabriel thrashed their bodies in pain as bites punctured and ripped through their fur.

A gull crash-landed with a squawk and Pip gasped as a swarm of Goliath Rats and Butcher Birds pinned it to the floor. As she thought desperately for a way to help it, a shrike dived with its sharp talons flexed. Pip ducked just in time and the Butcher Bird shrieked in frustration as it swooped upwards and returned to the tornado of shrikes and gulls battling above her in a terrifying uproar.

Pip darted across the floor and yelped as familiar cold, waxy claws clamped round her body and lifted her off the ground.

'It's all right, liddle lady, it's me,' GI Joe reassured her as Pip wriggled with panic inside his grasp. 'Let's get you outta this hornet's nest.'

GI Joe robustly flapped his wings and charged for the corridor leading out of the orphanage, but a moment later Pip's breath halted with fear. Through the throng of scuffling birds and rats, Lucia hurtled towards them.

'Look out!' Pip cried, and GI Joe swiftly swerved from her claws.

'She's mine!' the white pigeon growled, darting after him at once.

GI Joe tucked his wings into his body and plummeted through the air, but Lucia plunged after him at breakneck speed and snapped her beak at the little mouse tightly clasped in his talons.

As Pip flinched and dodged her biting jaws and GI Joe zigzagged through the whirlwind of seagulls and shrikes towards the hall leading out of the orphanage, suddenly

more bounding paws echoed off the walls, and Pip saw the silhouettes of Brian and Bing charge through the shadows. Over the Alsatians' heads, Philippe rocketed into the room, carrying Leo, scowling with determination, on his back.

'You stay away from her!' Leo roared as Philippe charged into Lucia and latched his strong claws round her right wing.

Knocking the flight from her, the white pigeon and the parrot spiralled through the air and hit the floor with a thump. GI Joe landed beside them and Pip met Leo's warm gaze. It was full of pride and her heart swelled to be near him again. A squeal sounded to their left and their eyes darted to Henri and the wolves, tussling with the mob of rats on the ground. A Goliath Rat flew from Gabriel's jaws and Pip shuddered at the number of rats and shrikes strewn across the floor. Her eyes searched the room for Madame Fourcade and she prayed she was safely out of harm's way with her hoglets.

'Get off me!' Lucia snarled, staggering to a stand.

Philippe's thick claws tightened round her and she tumbled to the ground. 'Kill them!' she shrieked, eyes roving wildly to the Butcher Birds and the Goliath Rats, but the battle between the shrikes and the seagulls was deafening and none heard her over the din. 'Kill them all!'

'Let her go, Philippe,' Leo said, staring up at Bing and Brian sprinting towards them with their lips curling back from their teeth. GI Joe's hackles rose, and Pip's blood thudded in her ears at seeing the sky-dogs' fury.

'Gladly,' the parrot squawked.

'It's over, Lucia,' GI Joe said. 'Your days of hurting us are finished.'

Pip knew Lucia's heart brimmed with venom and her quest for revenge would never cease. She had killed Hans and Léon and brought death and suffering to many more, yet Pip pitied her. To show Lucia mercy and risk her escaping and harming others was too dangerous, and she turned her head from the white pigeon, not wanting to see what would happen.

Bing and Brian pounced and an explosion of white feathers burst inside the assembly hall before gently floating to the parquet floor. Minutes later, the feverish scuffle of animals came to an end and, panting with throbbing grazes, bites and bruises, Henri, the wolves, the seagulls and the sky-dogs padded away from the abandoned house to meet their friends.

Ahead of them, Philippe and GI Joe followed the corridor leading out of the orphanage, and Pip gazed over her shoulder for one last glance at the umbrella, but she quickly looked away, the image of its shredded fabric and crumpled metal frame lying on the floor forever imprinted on her mind.

CHAPTER TWENTY-THREE

THE UMBRELLA

Stars shimmered above the orphanage as Pip was reunited with Madame Fourcade and her hoglets inside the stable, where they had remained hidden under the floorboard since Lucia and the Butcher Birds had taken her away.

'*Chérie!*' Madame Fourcade threw her paws round her with tears streaming down her cheeks. Christian and Béatrice took Pip's paws in theirs and smiled at the little mouse, their noses twitching. 'I don't know how I can ever repay you.'

'Lucia won't trouble us again.' Pip smiled, relieved to find Madame Fourcade and her hoglets safe and well. 'Bing and Brian have made sure of it.' Now that the fight was over and fear no longer pulsed through her limbs, she was consumed with exhaustion and felt the urgent sting of tears.

'You did a very brave thing facing her on your own like that,' GI Joe added, wrapping his wing round her shoulder. He drew her close, and Pip felt comforted by the warmth of his body against hers.

'A heroic thing,' Leo said earnestly as Philippe landed beside them. He dismounted from the parrot and rushed to Pip's side. 'We all owe you our lives, *topolina*.'

'I just did what I could.' Pip stared at the floor, not feeling proud of what had happened. The terror and violence of it would stay with her for the rest of her life. 'I couldn't let her hurt us any more.'

'*Ma petite chérie* –' Madame Fourcade's eyes darted about the animals, her brow furrowing with concern – 'where is your umbrella?'

A lump swelled in Pip's throat and she hung her head, trying to quiet the grief rising inside her. The umbrella had been with her since the day she was born, and she would miss it and Mama and Papa forever.

'Dammit,' GI Joe cursed, 'I'm sorry. I didn't think – I just wanted to get you outta there.'

'We all did.' Philippe sighed, flexing his wings and motioning his head to GI Joe. 'Let's go back and get it, GI.'

'Wait . . .' Pip's voice wavered and all her friends' faces fell. 'I had to let it go. I couldn't tell Lucia what I knew about Churchill's Secret Animal Army and the Resistance. The Butcher Birds and the Goliath Rats destroyed it. It's gone.'

Unable to stifle the urge to cry any longer, Pip covered her face with her paws and wept, and her friends enveloped her with kind embraces and sympathetic words. Behind them, Henri and the wolves stepped into the barn through the open stable door, with the Alsatians trotting after them and the seagulls flying over their heads.

Pip and her friends turned to the sound of claws pacing over the wooden floor and her breath caught in her throat, spotting Brian carrying the destroyed umbrella inside his jaws. Henri gently nudged Madame Fourcade with his nose and the hedgehog's face brightened, seeing her old friend return with the wolves, who gently licked her hoglets, hiding shyly behind their mother's quills.

'We're sorry, young Pip,' Bing said as Brian gently placed the umbrella on the ground beside her. The sky-dogs sat on their haunches as the seagulls settled around the barn and Pip sniffed, seeing its devastation. Its ornate silver handle was scratched and only a few tattered wisps of the canopy remained, revealing its bare, misshapen skeleton from where so many teeth, beaks and claws had ripped it apart.

'Wait a *momento* . . .' Leo carefully examined its dislocated spokes. 'This isn't so bad,' he said, realigning one segment after another. 'We can bend these ribs back into place and it should open again. Hmmm . . .' He scrunched up his face in thought. 'The handle is scraped –' his eyes pored over its structure from top to bottom – 'but it's not the end of the world. With new fabric, it will look better than ever.'

'Do you really think so?' Pip darted to his side, ears pricking with hope. She traced the naked umbrella frame with her paw and a rush of happiness tingled her fur, seeing that Leo was right.

'The men and women who work in the umbrella museum will fix it when we get to Italy,' Leo said. 'They'll make sure this one is well looked after. You'll see.'

'Have you been there?' Pip asked, her whiskers popping on her cheeks with surprise.

'*Si.*' Leo beamed, standing taller with pride. 'The artist I lived with used to sketch the parasols in the displays. I would sneak inside his pocket when he went on walks. I saw some beautiful umbrellas through his moth holes, but I never knew mice lived inside them. Philippe and I will take you there if you'd like us too, *topolina.*' Leo glanced up at the parrot nodding beside him. 'You'll need another bird to help you carry the umbrella, and, when the time is right, we'd be honoured to show you the way. The umbrella museum is on a wooded hill only a few miles from my village beside Lake Maggiore. We'll come and visit you when you are there.'

'Only if you take me exploring with you,' Pip said, feeling a weight lift inside her as she realized for the first time that she was nervous about her new life in the umbrella museum. But she immediately felt better knowing Leo and Philippe would be nearby.

Philippe winked. 'It's a deal.'

'But you and your umbrella must stay with me until Hitler's puppet, Mussolini, falls,' Madame Fourcade said firmly. 'It's not safe for you to travel to Italy until then, and I'm sure you, Christian and Béatrice will enjoy each other's company until that day comes. You all have the same courageous hearts,' the hedgehog continued with a sigh. 'My only fear is that, together, your combined mischief will turn my fur completely white!'

Pip grinned, wanting to spend as much time as she could with Madame Fourcade and her friends before she had to leave.

'I'll be staying with you too.' Henri smiled and Pip beamed at having him with her again.

'And me, liddle lady,' GI Joe cooed. 'I swore to Bernard Booth I'd keep you safe and you won't be getting rid of me until you're settled with your Italian family.'

'There's still much to be done,' Madame Fourcade said. 'We need to keep the enemy at bay and we must find and release any of our friends who may have been captured. We'll go back to the forest in Normandy and wait for the rest of Noah's Ark. Bernard Booth will be in touch with instructions. Together, we'll do what we can to bring an end to the war.'

A broad smile drew across Pip's lips as she felt a flutter of excitement for the time they had left together. The journey to the umbrella museum in Gignese was not over and none of them knew what lay ahead, but for now they were thankful this difficult chapter had closed.

The war was not won and many months of fighting were still to come, yet Pip and her friends had each other and the love they shared would stay with them forever.

EPILOGUE

Peter James Smith took his daughter's small hand in his and hopped up the stone steps to a pair of large glass doors that reflected the bright summer sky and his rented Fiat 500 parked on the hillside under the shade of tall cypress trees gently swaying in the northern Italian breeze.

'Come on, Gracie my love!' he said at the top of the steps, turning to his wife behind them, who was lifting their chubby young son to her hip. 'Last one inside is a nincompoop!'

Grace smiled with an affectionate roll of her eyes and joined her husband and daughter as they chuckled mischievously at the top of the stairs.

'Without further ado,' Peter said, pushing and holding the glass door open for his family to step inside, 'may I present to you, the Museo Dell'Ombrello – the only umbrella museum in the world.'

'Is this like the place where you grew up with Granny and Grandpa before the war?' his daughter said, letting go of his hand and running to get a closer look at the rows of umbrellas on display before them.

'Not quite.' He joined her in pressing his nose against the glass in front of a long line of ornate tasselled parasols. Beside them, photographs of Ancient Greek vases depicted men and women using them to shade themselves from the sun. 'The place I grew up was a shop, not a museum. We didn't sell old-fashioned sun parasols like these. We sold modern umbrellas that my father – your grandfather – made himself. People came from all over the world to buy them.'

'Were Granny and Grandpa's umbrellas as pretty as these ones?'

'Our canopies were not as intricate, but we did have beautiful handles carved into all sorts of things. Come on, let's see what else they have here.'

He took her hand in his and they walked around each display, looking at the first sun parasols from Ancient China, Egypt, Rome, India, Greece and Persia.

'Look,' Peter said, enthusiastically pointing to pictures fixed on the wall, and his daughter craned her neck to get a better look. 'In Siam, the monks used palm leaves for umbrellas and the Aztecs used canopies made out of feathers and gold!'

As they moved on, they passed more modern French, Italian and English umbrellas before they stopped in front of a cabinet in the far corner of the room, filled with beautifully sculpted wood, ebony, bone and silver handles.

'What can you see here?'

The little girl took a deep breath and spoke quickly, pointing to each carving with her finger.

'There's a dog, a parrot, a flower, a scary head with a hat on, a bear, another dog, a horse head, a snake, a tiger, a duck, a crocodile, a mouse – actually lots of mice!' She paused and looked up at her father, who was not listening to her and pressing the palms of his hands against the glass in astonishment. 'What is it, Daddy?'

'It's impossible.'

'What is, darling?' Grace said softly, placing her hand between his shoulder blades and furrowing her brow with concern. 'Are you all right?'

'That umbrella . . .' He pointed his finger to the display cabinet. 'The open one in the middle – I know it.'

'I'm sure lots of umbrellas look the same.'

'No, you don't understand,' he said, speaking quickly with excitement. 'This one was my mother's favourite in the shop – there simply *isn't* another one like it!'

'What do you mean, sweetheart?'

'Do you see the beautiful silver handle carved with fig leaves and inlaid with gold?' His wife nodded. 'It was given to the famous Jonas Hanway by the King of Persia while he was travelling there. It was originally meant to top a walking stick but Hanway added it to his umbrella in the mid-eighteenth century. It's said that he was the first man to use an umbrella in England.'

'Jonas Hanway the charity man?'

'Yes, he was the one who started the Marine Society, built the Magdalen Hospital and helped to stop the child chimney sweeps being used as slaves. Before he started using this umbrella every day, wealthy people were used to taking taxis when it rained. My parents talked about him all the time when I was growing up. This umbrella was their pride and joy.'

'They must have donated it to the museum before the bomb destroyed the shop.'

'Impossible. They wanted to come to the museum themselves after the war. I still have the letters my mother wrote to me about what time of year would be best for us to come here – she didn't want us to feel too hot. Besides, this umbrella was still at home on my last leave before D-Day.'

'Three weeks later the shop was gone. Could they have sent it ahead?'

'I don't think so. Not when Northern Italy was still an Axis territory.'

'Daddy,' his daughter said, insistently tugging on the end of his suit jacket, 'can we go and get some ice cream now?'

'In a minute, darling,' he said, staring rapt at the umbrella. 'Why don't you ask Mummy?'

'*Please*, Daddy! You promised we would get ice cream after we looked at the umbrellas!'

'All right,' he said, turning to his wife with an innocent face that betrayed a hint of a mischievous smile. 'I'll meet you there in a minute.'

His wife eyed him suspiciously.

'Ice cream!' cried the little boy in her arms.

'Come on, Mummy,' her daughter said, bossily taking her free hand and pulling her to the museum exit on the other side of the large room. 'Today, I'd like a pink scoop, a white scoop and a green scoop.'

'Goodness! Certainly not!' Grace said firmly, pulling the large glass door open and walking into the bright sunshine with her children. 'One scoop is plenty.'

His daughter's pleading voice faded behind the door, swinging closed behind them. Carefully looking about him to check no one could see what he was about to do, Peter lifted the metal latch at the bottom corner of the glass display cabinet and pulled it slightly ajar. Feeling in his pocket, he found a little domed chocolate coated in silver paper dotted with blue stars that the hotel waiter had given him after dinner the night before. He unwrapped it, broke off a piece in his fingers and slipped his hand inside the cabinet to leave the chocolate beside the Hanway umbrella handle. Drawing his hand out again, he closed the door and waited, his heart thudding inside his chest.

Minutes passed and Peter sighed with disappointment, turning to leave. But then he saw it in the corner of his eye. Moving slowly and stealthily, often pausing motionless against the silver fig-leaf carvings on the umbrella handle, a tiny mouse kitten clambered to the chocolate and picked it up in its little paws.

'It can't be!' he said, leaping back to the display. But at once he clenched his jaw and scolded himself with a shake of his head. 'It's impossible! She'd be fully grown by now, probably even dead. For goodness sake, man! Get a grip! What did you expect? How on earth would she even get to Italy in the first place?'

At that moment, a shrill squeak sounded and the kitten looked up into the canopy. Just visible, another bigger mouse with a white underbelly hung upside down by its tail with its paws on its hips.

'*Could* it be her?' he whispered to himself, seeing the mouse's familiar white stomach and gasping with delight. 'My God – I think it is!'

Without a doubt, it was the same mouse he knew from long ago inside the umbrella shop. As the kitten dashed up the umbrella handle to join its mother inside the canopy, Peter distinctly heard disapproving squeaks and chatter. He pressed his ear to the cool glass, wishing he could understand what she was saying.

'Hans! I told you *not* to leave the umbrella during the day!' Pip scolded as two other kittens leaned over her shoulder with their noses twitching inquisitively. 'It's not safe!'

'But you left London and brought the umbrella all the way here,' her son said defensively, leaping over the metal stretchers to their family nest at the highest point of the umbrella. As he broke the chocolate into small pieces, he shared the treat between him, his mother and his two sisters and they nibbled it greedily. 'That's much more dangerous!'

'That was different – we were at war.'

'Tell us the story about the Dickin the rescue dog again, Mama,' Pip's youngest kitten said, her little cheeks bulging with chocolate.

'Not that one! I want to hear how you met Papa when you were fighting in the Battle for Paris and how you saved the

Eiffel Tower!' her oldest daughter squeaked. 'It's so romantic!'

'Boring! I want to hear about Noah's Ark!' Hans said. 'Especially about the pigeon, the eagle and the hedgehog!'

'And the stag and Hans the German rat,' her daughters pleaded, 'and the sky-dogs! And the white mouse!'

'All right.' Pip smiled as she lifted her youngest kitten to her knee while the other two nestled beside her, and she began her story in the same way she always did. 'Once upon a time when the world was mad with war . . .'

'Mama,' Hans interrupted, his nose twitching in thought, 'if we went to war again, would we have to move the umbrella and find a new home like you did?'

'That would depend on what options we had. But we would have to choose carefully – after all, the choices you make can lead you down very different paths that you can't always come back from.'

'We won't go to war again, will we, Mama?' her youngest asked, with drooping whiskers and her little brow furrowing with worry.

'I hope very much that we will never go to war again. It was a despicable time of suffering and hatred,' Pip said with a sad shake of her head, and a lump suddenly swelled in her throat as she remembered all those she had lost. As she collected herself with a sigh, she looked fondly at each of her children with the same wise expression that her own mother had given her, long ago. 'The most important thing is that we never forget what happened. Every one of us must teach our kittens about our mistakes and how to fix them so they never occur again.'

'But how do we know it won't happen again?' her oldest daughter squeaked.

'We don't. All we can do is learn from the past and try our best to make each day a kinder day than yesterday. Life is difficult and you will have many challenges in your lives, but with courage in your hearts you can be the change we need for a better tomorrow – and you'll never fail because you will have tried your best to make that happen.'

Suddenly Peter jumped with surprise away from the glass cabinet, feeling a determined yank at his sleeve.

'Hurry up, Daddy,' his daughter bossed with a halo of melted ice cream round her lips. 'We're missing you!'

'All right,' he said, lifting her into his arms and kissing her cheek. Drawing a handkerchief from his top jacket pocket, he tenderly wiped her face. 'I'm coming.'

Walking towards his wife and son, patiently waiting outside with their ice creams, Peter shook his head in disbelief and smiled, wondering about the little mouse's

 adventures, delighted to think that the most extraordinary things can happen to the smallest of creatures.

 THE END

AUTHOR'S NOTE

Umbrella Mouse to the Rescue is set during the final months of WWII and follows the events surrounding the Liberation of Paris in August 1944. It is just one story featuring members of the real French Resistance and this note explains some of the facts behind Pip's adventure but there are countless other stories to be discovered.

Both the Umbrella Mouse books coincide with Operation Overlord that began with D Day on 6th June 1944 and ended on 30th August 1944 with German forces retreating east across the river Seine after their defeat at the Battle of Falaise and the Liberation of Paris. *Umbrella Mouse to the Rescue* ends with the dramatic battle for Paris, during which a verbal ceasefire between the Allied and Axis forces was instated. This bought time for the Resistance to convince the Allies to come to the fight. It also gave German troops time to retreat. The truce officially ended on 22nd August 1944. Over the next three days, more than 600 barricades appeared across the city. When the Allied armies arrived in Paris on the night of 24th August, all the church bells rang in the city for the first time since 1940, beginning with Notre-Dame.

The fire inside the Grand Palais witnessed by Pip and her friends, started on 23rd August after German Goliath tanks attacked it. Artistic license has let me compress the timeline and bend the truth on other events during that period. Most notably, the Eiffel Tower was never rigged with explosives. Hitler demanded that Paris be destroyed, but General von Choltitz, a commander in Paris, did not have the weaponry to do so. Only the telephone exchange and the Saint-Cloud Bridge were ever mined. Von Choltitz is sometimes known as a 'saviour of Paris' for refusing to carry out Hitler's orders. Historians argue whether or not the city would have survived if he'd had the necessary arsenal. In fact, Paris was remarkably undamaged during WWII due to its swift defeat in 1940, never suffering a Blitz. Researching in Paris, I visited the mysterious and atmospheric catacombs. I have found no evidence of the Resistance using the limestone labyrinth, although Colonel Rol's nearby civil defence shelter did house bicycle generators used during powercuts, but I couldn't resist including this dark hideout beneath the city – perfect for my band of Resistance animals.

Madame Fourcade was the leader of a vast intelligence network of nearly 3,000 men and women working to support the French Resistance, who were given the nickname 'Noah's Ark' by the Gestapo because they used animal codenames. My first book, *The Umbrella Mouse*, will introduce you to many of these brave people who I've reimagined in animal form. Madame Fourcade's children, Christian (aged 12) and Béatrice (10) were targeted by the Gestapo and had their own daring escape from France into Switzerland in 1943. Madame Fourcade herself was in Paris in August 1944 and organized the delivery of intelligence revealing the enemy as weaker than rumours circulating at the time, but wasn't in the city for the liberation.

Nor was the real life New Zealander Nancy Wake, whose ability to evade capture earned her the nickname 'the white mouse'. To my knowledge, she never met or communicated with Madame Fourcade or Noah's Ark, who reported intelligence to MI6 while Nancy coordinated sabotage for the Special Operations Executive (SOE), including aiding and training part of the Maquis – rural bands of guerrilla French Resistance fighters that operated all over France. She was the only woman amongst thousands of men and she became one of the most decorated heroines of WWII. Madame Fourcade also spent time with the Maquis who sheltered her shortly after she had escaped capture by squeezing through the bars of her cell in July 1944. *Le Maquis* means 'thicket', hence the bramble hideout that is sadly destroyed in *Umbrella Mouse to the Rescue*.

My Maquis includes some key members of the real-life Noah's Ark who were not Maquisards: Ferdinand Rodriquez (codename 'Magpie'), Monique Bontinck ('Ermine') – they married each other after the war – and Gabriel Rivière ('Wolf') and his wife Madeleine. They appear here so I could give them weightier roles. Gabriel was executed on 21st August 1944. 'Spider' was executed at Natzweiler-Struthof, aged 21. Marguerite de Macmahon ('Firefly') was another member of Noah's Ark who had to flee France. Pregnant, she crawled under barbed wire into Switzerland with her three children. Noah's Ark was truly betrayed by an agent codenamed 'Canary' in 1942.

In France, wolves were hunted to extinction in the 1930s and did not return until the 1990s. Gabriel and Madeline's den near Louviers was inspired by the Louviers wolf from the 16th century. The secret phrases Madame Fourcade exchanges with them were announced on Radio Londres, a station that broadcasted coded messages to the French Resistance.

Noor, my kingfisher radio-operator, is based on the British SOE heroine, Noor Inayat Kahn, who made a failed escape attempt with Noah's Ark's Léon Faye in 1943. Like him, she vanished under Hitler's secret *Nacht und Nebel* punishment for resistance fighters. Noor was executed at Dachau on 13th September 1944. She is a kingfisher because I think they are extraordinary.

GI Joe was not recruited into the pigeon service until 1943 and he was not at the D-Day landings. I do not know where he or Lucia di Lammermoor were at the time of these events. The sky-dogs, Bing and Brian, are inspired by two of the three dogs that parachuted into Normandy on D-Day with the 13th (Lancashire) Parachute Battalion. There is conflicting evidence as to whether Bing and Brian is one dog called Brian with the nickname 'Bing' or two different dogs. Two appear in *Umbrella Mouse to the Rescue* due to War Office records for Brian (War-Dog 2720/6871) and Bing (War-Dog 2738/6218). Either way, Brian won a Dickin Medal for bravery. I like to think of them being friends. Both survived the war.

I read many amazing books in my research for Pip's adventures. For example, *The Secret Agent's Pocket Manual 1939–1945* taught me that saboteurs plugged wax into punctured fuel lines, but as a method of starting an engine fire. I read in *Smithsonian Magazine* that sphagnum moss was used in WWI to treat wounds. Madame Fourcade's own memoir, *Noah's Ark* set me on this journey in the first place. There are so many fantastic resources you can use to research the period of history that interests you most and wonderful stories can come from them. I hope I have done these exceptional animals and people justice. They all deserve to be remembered.

ACKNOWLEDGEMENTS

Seeing *The Umbrella Mouse* in bookshops across the country and in people's hands both in person and online has made the last year one of the best (and most surreal) I've ever had. Thank you to everyone who has bought it, every bookseller, librarian and teacher who has championed it, every reader, journalist, reviewer and blogger who has shouted about it. I am beyond grateful. *Umbrella Mouse to the Rescue* is for you.

I still have to pinch myself that the little story I wrote on my phone during my commute on the London Underground has come this far. Huge thanks to my agent, Chloe Seager, for seeing something in Pip and me in the first place, and her enduring support, kindness, wisdom, dedication and dry wit. And to the rest of the team at Madeleine Milburn – you are a lovely bunch to know. To my editor, Lucy Pearse, for her encouragement, intelligence, insight and imagination, and for believing in *The Umbrella Mouse* in such a way that now there is also *Umbrella Mouse to the Rescue*. To everyone at Macmillan Children's Books for everything they have done for me, especially Jo Hardacre, Kat McKenna, Emma Quick, Sarah Clarke, Emily Bromfield, Sabina Maharjan and Corinne Gotch. To Samantha Stewart for copy-editing and to Nick de Somogyi for proofreading. To Sam Usher, an extraordinary illustrator.

To my grandfather, Squadron Leader Thomas Philip Fargher, Marie-Madeleine Fourcade, her children Christian and Béatrice, Noah's Ark, Nancy Wake and the Dickin Medal winning animal heroes whose incredible experiences have inspired Pip's adventures.

To Waterstones for making *The Umbrella Mouse* your Book of the Month and giving it the best exposure a debut author could hope for. I will never forget seeing your windows adorned with cuddly mice and yellow umbrellas and I am forever thankful. To all your booksellers, Sue Chambers, Meg Burrows, Becca Wynde for organizing events and Fiona Sharp for nudging Disney to make a movie!

To my local independent booksellers in Suffolk: Johnny and Mary James at Aldeburgh Bookshop and Catherine Larner at Browsers Bookshop in Woodbridge.

To Sainsbury's and Book Trust for giving *The Umbrella Mouse* your fiction prize in 2019.

To all the authors who have been so kind: Michael Morpurgo, Gill Lewis and Claire Fayers for their quotes, and to all the other supportive authors I have come to know both in life and online. To Mel Taylor-Bessent for having me on Authorfy.

To James Smith & Sons Umbrellas in London. Thank you for backing *The Umbrella Mouse* even though I blew up your shop in 1944, which never happened.

To Matthew Cobb for writing *Eleven Days in Paris* that informed the historical context of this book. To Lynn Olson for her biography, *Madame Fourcade's Secret War*, which was published in the UK just after *The Umbrella Mouse* and expanded upon Madame Fourcade's truncated and badly translated memoir, *Noah's Ark*.

To Christopher Beaver (late 1ˢᵗ The Queen's Dragoon Guards) for answering various battlefield queries from muzzle flash to explosive detonators. To my sister in law, Sophie Fargher, for checking my German insults. To Karlo Zelencic, for helping me with my Australian slang. To Sally Walton for generously letting me stay in her Paris flat for a week while I was researching. To Jonathan Holt at the Tank Museum, who helped me figure out Tiger tanks. To Steven P Wickstrom for answering my questions about herring gulls. To Cressi Downing, Clare Povey and James Rennoldson from Writers & Artists for encouraging me when I doubted myself at the very start of this journey.

To my parents Tim and Lizzie and my siblings Zoë, Matthew and Ed. I'm extremely lucky to have you. To my husband James, my heart. To the rest of my family and friends, I'm so glad I know you.

And to you dear reader. Thank you for joining me for Pip's last hurrah. I really hope you've enjoyed yourselves as much as I have.

ABOUT THE AUTHOR

Anna Fargher was raised in a creative hub on the Suffolk coast by an artist and a ballet teacher. She read English Literature at Goldsmiths before working in the British art world and opening her own gallery. *The Umbrella Mouse* was her first book, which she wrote on her phone's notepad during her daily commute on the London Underground. It was the winner of the Sainsbury's Children's Book Prize for Fiction and selected as Children's Book of the Month in Waterstones.

Anna lives in London and Suffolk.

ABOUT THE ILLUSTRATOR

Sam Usher graduated from the University of West England and his debut picture book *Can You See Sassoon?* was shortlisted for the Waterstones Prize and the Red House Children's Book Award. He is particularly admired for his technical drawing skill and prowess with watercolour. Also a talented pianist, when he's not holding a pen and wobbling it at paper, you'll find him perfecting a fiendishly difficult piece of Chopin.

DISCOVER WHERE
THE ADVENTURE BEGAN

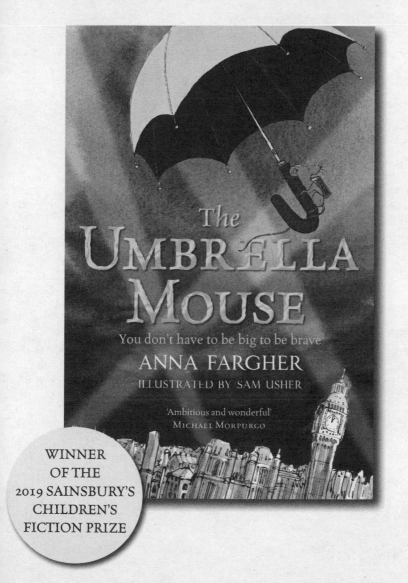

WINNER OF THE 2019 SAINSBURY'S CHILDREN'S FICTION PRIZE